THE BEACH IN WINTER

LESLIE PIKE

Nichole Strauss, Insight Editing Services
Virginia Carey, Proofreading
Kari March, Kari March Designs

For Don, who in death teaches me the final lessons of our love.

CHAPTER 1

PARISH

*T*he wind's begun to moan, interrupting my attempt at passing out. I sneer at Mother Nature's lame shot at keeping me conscious. Although I doubt she'd be turning her attention to one man whose goal it is to be invisible.

Besides, there's an even chance I'm imagining the whole scene. The abandoned lighthouse under an inky sky of blurred stars. The wild sea. Even the sharp smell of salty air. They could all be figments of a pickled brain. Delusion's become my preferred state.

Three a.m. is for writers who can't sleep. Their minds filled with words for someone who's not there. Or for people hoping to drink themselves into amnesia. Or in my case, both. I'm lost in this ocean of sorrow. And I keep drowning.

Concentrating on bringing the bottle into focus, I carefully raise it to my lips and take a long pull of whiskey. Familiar heat slides down my throat, while the rest of me shivers in the night air. The nearly empty fifth gets propped in the damp sand. Careful. Don't knock it over. There's still a few mouthfuls to be had before I lose myself. It would suck to have a tongue full of sand like last week. Or was it the week before?

A pile of tangled seaweed props me up. I was too wasted to go the extra six feet to the dune. There's a twisted piece of driftwood for my head to rest against. A hard pillow with knots in it suits the mood. The voice of the raging waves begins to carry me away. Here it comes. Hurry.

Today was bad. My mind has become the enemy. Once a strength, now it's relentless in its pursuit to make me remember, replay. A punishing fucking adversary who won't be silenced.

I've stopped begging God for compassion. There's been no response. Or maybe I misjudged Him and his quality of mercy. Could be His answer was, *Fuck you, get over it.*

And exactly who am I pleading with? I don't believe in a God anymore. I've seen no proof of a loving deity. It's a desperate man's last hope when there's nowhere else to turn. I'm past that.

No matter what I've tried, I can't stop thinking about my boy. How he could make me laugh more than anyone else. The blond curls that rested on his forehead like a cherub. Even when he was eight. And the expression he wore whenever I'd suggest a surfing trip.

It was always just the two of us. That's part of the pain. He had already missed out on so much in his short life. The crueler memories are too devastating to think about. I try not to hold those in my mind any longer than they demand.

What I'd give to shut down the images that play on. But it seems to be getting worse. Is it really too much to ask for relief after all these years? Whatever sentence I was handed by destiny must be served by now.

Maybe someday I'll write about the struggle. How I never recovered from the loss of my child. An instant best seller noted for its piercing insight. It'll be published posthumously, and everyone who ever knew me will say my suicide was inevitable.

That's no bullshit.

My lids lower. Then slowly lift. Lower. Open. Who's that standing on Happy Family's deck? A woman I haven't seen before. It's definitely not Babe. There's no sign of her Honey either. Sam

Boy must be with them. It's been at least a month since I've seen any of them.

There's only been those four unfamiliar men who stayed a weekend. I remember thinking how odd it was that none of them ever came down to the beach. Strange now that almost every light in the two-story house burns bright. And the rooms look different. Rearranged.

The writer in me reads the scene. Even through my haze and a hundred yards away, the body language says the woman's troubled. Or maybe it's exhaustion, head hanging as she braces herself on the rail. Somehow she looks out of place. Is there crying? Can't really tell from here. She's not dressed appropriately for the beach. Let alone late at night. Obviously, she comes from some other place.

I can't hold my eyes open anymore, so I cover them with my old favorite cap and give in to the darkness.

Soft Break

The seagull's departing caw startles me awake. At the same time, its loose shit splats on my cheek and runs back into my ear. The cap gets tossed aside.

"Crap!" I yell, ignoring the irony.

A double hit from that asshole with wings. The weird marking on the underbelly makes him stand apart. It's become his thing. And an existential metaphor for the state of my life. Yeah, I see you fucker. Even through this fog.

Where'd this come from? There's a blanket on me, feet to chin. Who did that? A whiff of my own puke crusted in the fabric reaches my nose. Disgusting. Hope whoever put this on me wasn't around when I hurled. Actually, what do I care?

Okay, it was a kindness, but one I wouldn't want again. *Mind your own fucking business, people.* Next time I'll move further down the beach against the cliffs.

I wipe my face with the only other thing available, a sleeve. The cap goes back onto my head. Standing, I feel like an old man.

Back, knees, reminding me they used to feel a lot differently. When I was running and swimming in the ocean every day, things were remarkably otherwise. Forty-three feels older than I knew it could. Truthfully, every part of me hurts. Maybe it's punishment. But from whom?

Turning toward the house, the familiar march back to my staircase begins. Every day. Every fucking day. My head's pounding and my mouth feels like the Sahara if it was covered in dog shit. I pick up the empty whiskey bottle as I pass. It's a laughable habit, drawing the line at littering.

I drag the blanket behind as my bare feet dig into the coarse sand of the Maine coastline. It's hard not to think of another beach, a softer sand. Above all, a kinder world.

When I look up, Sam Boy's watching. He stands on the deck, staring. You'd think he'd look away, but no. Neither of us smile. It's not like we're friends, but whenever we'd pass on the beach we almost always gave a nod.

He doesn't want to talk to the weird neighbor, and I have no interest in making meaningless conversation with a sour-faced kid. Hopefully the parents have told him to steer clear of the drunk. They should have. The very minimum required works for us both.

It feels like we're daring the other to look away. I'm not the only stubborn guy here. Someone must be calling from the house. His shoulders fall. He lifts his chin and listens for a few moments then turns and slowly goes inside. Interesting. This isn't like him at all.

The kid's led a charmed life. I saw how his parents enjoyed the sandcastles stage. Actually, I watched a few times then stopped. Too painful. That was when he was much younger and reminded me of Justin. Now I've taken to looking again. He's a teenager, or about to be. Thankfully he bears no resemblance to my child.

For him it's skimmer days. Childhood toys have been abandoned. He and his friend like to surf the sand dunes with boogie boards. In another life I would have liked doing that myself. These waters are too wild for actual surfing. Hell, you can't even swim here. That was something that drew me.

Didn't want this beach to remind me of our California one. Redondo Beach, California and Martin's Beach, Maine are diametrical opposites. It isn't just the texture of the sand that's different. There was bright sunshine three hundred days of the year in the old life. Here, just as many cold.

It's obvious that Sam prefers his friend's company to his parents now. There's always that one kid hanging with him. They inhabit the world between boy and man. I remember that age well. It was great. Carefree. Thoughts of my boyhood friends crowd my mind. I abandoned them too.

Wonder what's going on with this kid, though? The dark expression isn't normal. There seems to have been a sea change. Maybe I'm reading too much into the whole thing. He probably didn't get the new skateboard he wants. Or maybe it's a phone now. He's about that age.

Taking my stairs slowly, I give the kid one last look and a nod. It goes unreturned. Don't know why I did that. Except for the small part of me that thinks he really needed it.

I use the hose to wash the sand off my feet, then swing the unlocked door open and step back into my inner sanctum. I survived another night. A sigh escapes my lips like a relief valve followed by a putrid burp.

People who only know me as the unconscious man on the beach would be surprised to see how I live. Ordered shelves of books from floor to ceiling, the organized wooden desk with the Mac and my last novel sitting next to it. They're waiting for me, as if conscious of my routine.

What a turn in my professional life. Two best sellers as P.J. Adams at the beginning of my career. Before the tragedy stole everything. Even my name. I had to abandon it once every interviewer prodded me for details of how I was feeling. There was blood in the water, and it would always be that way.

As far as the public goes, that man has fallen off the face of the earth. No one ever called me Parish because I was P.J. from the time I was a kid. And Adams is such a common name. Early on, my publisher realized I'd go somewhere else in a hot minute if she didn't agree to go along with my plan. I'd write using the name Parish. One name only. I figured if Cher and Sting could do it, so could I. And interviews would never be granted.

My books made and continue to make too much money for her or anyone to argue the point.

Readers and critics haven't connected the dots because the genre has changed and with it the tone of my writing. Anonymity was the goal. Now P.J. Adams only exists within these walls, hidden on the shelves of neatly stacked books, far away from Parish detective stories.

Everything in its place. So opposite my inner life. An analyst would love to dissect that one. But I don't need any doctor explaining my behavior. These surroundings are the only things I'm capable of controlling in a world where random chaos happens. It's as simple and complex as that. There. Saved myself a couple of hundred dollars a session.

The blanket gets tossed on the washing machine as I pass the laundry closet in the hall. A shower's going to wash away the stink rising from my body. And maybe it'll clear the heaviness that's been hard to shake lately. No mystery what's prompting it. Every year in the lead up to the holidays, followed by his birthday, I go darker. This time it started earlier and it's more intense.

How sad to imagine Justin older when that's never going to be. In my fantasies we're always great friends. I'm the cool dad and all his friends want to come to our house. Strange how detailed an illusion can be.

This place is my only respite from the mess that's my life. At least I'm hidden here from prying eyes and concerned people who mean well. Keeping my acquaintances to a bare minimum helps. Random hookups are in hotel rooms. Marty at the bar is about the only person I talk to at any length, and it's only a few times a year and mostly sports related. But even he isn't welcome here.

It's not a home in the standard definition. That requires lots more than one occasionally warm body. At the very least you should be interested in making it your own. Putting your stamp on things. But here only the top drawer of the desk tells my story.

Eight hundred seventy-five feet and no second bedroom discourages visitors. Not that anyone knows where I am. But in the age of the Internet, you can be found. My brother and sister must have tried, even though they don't admit to it when we talk. Over the years I've steered them away from any conversations that involve the past, my state of mind, Justin, or the possibility of a visit.

I think they're afraid our once-a-year phone call will stop. But I can't do more. I just can't. I'd be afraid my sadness would pull them down with me. If it came to it, I'd put up a *No Trespassers* sign and enforce it.

Soft Break

At least I smell better. The bar that measures a good day for me is set remarkably low. Every morning I try to reboot. Leave the night behind and begin again. Let go of the dark thoughts and the indulgences while there's daylight. It's the only way I'm surviving, searching for small signs I'm making progress. But so far they haven't showed up. I keep hoping one day will be better.

The morning light helps get me in the right frame of mind to write. Four weeks till my deadline. Then I'll start outlining the next one. I still remember the break between books I took a few years ago. That was a fucking mistake. Filling my days with another man's plot twists is the only way to temporarily escape my own.

Good thing the imagination's as vivid as ever, because I've got to rely on it exclusively. My world has shrunk, and with it my ability to keep as current as I should. I don't watch much television or take the newspaper. There's too many opportunities for me to be reminded of that day. Too many new survivors of fresh terrors whose eyes look like mine. The world has become even crueler.

Instead, I Google what I need to know or want to learn. It's specific and I can avoid the things I need to turn from. I used to love discovering the new. Cultures, people, food. Philosophies. Not anymore. Routine is the only way forward. Come up from the beach, masturbate in the shower, put on a fresh pair of boxer briefs and one of my oversized sweaters. Wet hair, spent dick, coffee, and whatever's left over from the week's grocery shopping. Today it's an overripe banana and a hard piece of salami.

In another life I liked cooking. I was good at it, in fact. Justin loved what I'd make for him, and when he was a toddler he'd hold out his hands and open and close his fingers till I'd bring him more. He went through a stage where he'd cry when it was gone.

It used to drive me crazy thinking that whenever his mother had him his diet consisted of fast food crap. She couldn't even care for him properly for forty-eight hours at a time. That was before I got full custody. Shit. Now I'm thinking of Marsha, which only leads to more negative thoughts. And not just of her. I carry as much blame because I was old enough to know better. Screwing a random woman in a club while foregoing a condom isn't a great idea.

Setting the coffee on the desk, I take my seat and look out at the dark jewel-colored sea. That's why I bought this place. The wall of glass and the scene before it. The endless expanse of an ever-changing ocean.

Most days I spend time standing on the beach staring at the waves rising and slamming with such force they actually make the ground shake. There's always an undercurrent of rage in the Atlantic, even on its mildest day. I like that.

I haven't been in the ocean for five years. Never would have believed it. Now I'm just an armchair surfer imagining epic rides.

I can't see any neighbors from this vantage point. No one can see me through the darkened glass. I'd have to go on the deck and peek around the corner of the house to be able to spot Happy Family's home and the one further down the beach closest to it.

On the opposite end, the house closest to mine is much further away. Almost to the lighthouse. It's dark and kind of spooky, with iron lanterns that glow at night. Looks like a fortress for Dracula.

In reality, a nice older man lives there. The lighthouse keeper. That's what he said to call him the one time we had an actual conversation. I've shortened it to LK. Marty told me the guy owns half the beach property. Bought fifty years ago when no one wanted to live on a secluded beach, not made for swimming.

Okay, get it over with. Quit looking out the window. It's not going anywhere, and I need to finish the epilogue. First, a sip of steaming coffee from my Stanford University mug. I pull the drawer open, and my eyes dart to the letters first. Two sealed envelopes with the names of my sister and brother, Gayle and John. I leave them facing up, names showing, so they won't be overlooked if the worst happens.

It wouldn't be the worst for me, but it would for them. The thought of my siblings' broken hearts is the only thing holding me back lately. That and the fact you can't commit suicide if you're already dead.

My gaze moves to the picture always left facedown. It would be a mistake to see his image without first steeling myself. Every day it's the same thing. I pick it up and turn it toward me. Joy and unspeakable sorrow mix to make this feeling I'm well acquainted with. People say grief changes into something new. Not gone, but something palatable. Really? Five years later I'm still waiting.

This is the one image of him I allow myself to look at. All the others are on flash drives stored in a safe deposit box at the bank.

9

Precious unbearable memories. As soon as I can look at the one I allow myself and not fall apart, then I'll look at the others.

I smile a bit at the expression on his face. Turning the picture over, I read the familiar words. *Redondo Beach 2008.*

He was just three.

I run my finger over his face as if it can be considered touching. In the image he's got ahold of my hands and we're about to jump the tiny wave that rolls toward the shore. Can't remember who took the shot. Must have been my mother.

The moment's frozen forever. You can tell he thinks the wave's huge. But he's giggling because he trusted me. *Daddy would save him from every danger and all the monsters.* My shoulders droop with the thought of how wrong he was.

Muted voices carrying from the beach bring me back to the present. When I lift my head, I see Sam Boy and his female companion walking this way. Not sure what's being said, but Boy's getting agitated. His index finger points in my direction. What the hell's that about? Then his hand's in the air making some kind of frustrated point.

The woman's demeanor matches his. She was calm at first. That's changing. They're both talking at once. Then in a gesture of what looks like pent-up anger, the kid picks up a rock and throws it as hard as he can in the direction of the sea. She looks stymied as to how to respond. Hmm. I can use that bit. Besides, it's none of my business. I've got writing to do.

I jot down a few key words on my pad next to the computer so I'll remember to include it in the next novel. A glimpse of body language that says more than words. I'm a collector of bits of human nature gleaned while watching walkers and runners and occasional fog worshippers. Many have shown up in my *Daniel Dustin* series. The private detective lives on a beach I pretend isn't this one. My own loner tendencies have become his. And he's just as fucked up as I am. The fans connect with that. Readers love a flawed character.

CHAPTER 2

SCARLETT

"Cut me a break!" I call to the departing figure. My obvious frustration with him escaping in a high-pitched voice.

This damn sand. Running after someone on it isn't the easiest thing. His young legs are outdistancing me. Even when you're in your thirties, thirteen has the advantage. To add to the picture, my boobs are bouncing like two rubber balls. An imaginary drumbeat sounds somewhere counting out the rhythm. Where did I pack the sports bra? I look like a goon wobbling my way forward.

Montana's big sky has never been missed so desperately. This scene, this spot on earth, seems to be the polar opposite. Contained and all in grey tones. Maybe I'm judging it too quickly. But this friggin place is depressing. My bad attitude this early in our new normal isn't a good sign.

It's possible I may have lost some of my credibility with Sam as well. I can't picture my sister or brother in law having to chase their son and beg him to listen. They were always good at communicating and in charge. They wouldn't have put up with this behavior. Never did I see Sam have attitude with his parents. Well he's got one toward his Aunt Scarlett. That didn't take long.

Can it really be only ten in the morning on day two? Besides that, it's cold as shit and I stepped on a broken shell a few minutes ago. Is that blood? Fuck my life. There. I admitted to myself what can never be said aloud. Not without me sounding like an asshole.

Sam turns to face me and his blue-eyed gaze doesn't blink. You don't have to be psychic to see the kid's angry and at the same time incredibly sad. I get it. I am too. Neither of us asked for this. Who do I rail against?

"I'll go get it myself," he says harshly. "I don't need you."

Turning away, his voice trails off with the last declaration, knowing he hit his mark.

"I don't know much about taking care of a kid," I call following him, "but I know not to let a thirteen-year-old go to a house of a man who passes out drunk on the beach!"

"You should have thought about that when you gave away *my* blanket."

Little shithead. We reach the steps to the drunken man's home and I place my hand on Sam's shoulder. He stops.

"Wait. Come on. We're both on edge. Let's take a breath," I say, trying a calmer tone.

He softens the scowl, and a deep sigh seals our shaky truce.

"What about I buy you a new blanket? A better one. That one was kind of worn," I offer.

A veil of sadness falls over his sweet face and with it a frustrated shake of the head. *What did I say wrong?*

"Mom gave me that when I was little. I just wanted to keep it."

Oh, shoot me now. Crap.

"I'm sorry, Sam. I didn't know. Of course you want to keep it."

"Then you'll get it back? Because if you don't, I will."

The kid's got balls.

Looking up the stairs to the man's front door, I hesitate for just a beat.

"Yeah. Okay, I'll try. But you stay here."

Sam saves any further argument for another time. He made the most compelling one anyway. I climb the stairs and try coming up with a sound plan. I'll introduce myself and just tell the truth.

How can any reasonable person deny a boy his deceased mother's gift? Yeah that'll work.

Sam's sure he saw the guy dragging it back to his house. Hope he didn't chuck it already. I should have thought ahead and brought gloves or a plastic bag. The poor man could have pissed on it and now I'll have to touch the thing. Who knows what kind of bacteria I'm going to be dealing with? Has anyone ever gotten a sexually transmitted disease from touching urine? My luck I'd be patient zero.

The narrow deck is nearly bare, except for one well-used chair and the patina-colored metal table beside it. It holds an ashtray filled with crushed butts. He misses it often enough to litter the deck. I count at least six half smoked Marlboros strewn across the wood, none of which have been stepped on. Some have long ashes still attached. It's as if they fell from his hand while he passed out.   ⎯   ⎯

This guy has a death wish. Cigarettes, booze. Sam said he's slept on the beach a few times, but that becoming unconscious is a new thing. New or not, his habits will eventually put him out of his misery. Whatever that may be. I've got my own problems to obsess about.

As I approach the door, the faint outline of a tall male figure is visible through the darkened glass. He's standing to the left of the entry. Details aren't sharp but there's someone there, and he's looking my way. Yikes. There's something long and baggy on top, but I don't think he's wearing pants because I can make out an outline of his calves.

The more I stare the surer I am those are bare legs. Good ones but unadorned. Oh great. Am I about to be greeted by a half-naked man? Figures it would be the important half. He stands perfectly still, watching as I ring the bell. Creepy. I take one step back.

There's no movement or reaction to the sound. He watches while I decide what to do next.

"Um, hello?" I call through the door.

Nothing. I raise my voice.

"My name is Scarlett Lyon. I'm Sam's aunt and I just moved in next door. I don't mean to bother you, but I need to ask for that blanket back. I left it with you last night. My nephew has informed me it's very important to him. I'm sure you can understand."

Nothing. Now he's pissing me off.

I wave to the ghost behind the glass. He steps back. "I can see you standing there. Is there a chance we might talk?" I say pointedly.

There's a pause then he slowly moves closer. The door opens, but only enough for me to see one bloodshot brown eye framed by a thick dark eyebrow and half a face peeking out. The body's hidden. Wow. Half's enough. Shocking really. Drunken mess of a man's handsome, with a wet head of thick black hair. Not to mention the sexy stubble. I suddenly recall my weakness for flawed men.

Watch yourself, Scarlett.

In any other circumstance I'd be plotting how I was going to get him to notice me. Right now I'm wishing I wore something other than this unappealing gray sweatshirt, black sweatpants, and generic ponytail. For the first time in my life I forgot to brush my teeth and skipped the deodorant. Great timing.

But come on. Am I really critiquing myself instead of the guy? I shouldn't forget I know too much about the man, and it's more than a minor flaw. It's a deal breaker. My line in the sand. Literally. I should take a stick and draw a line around his property. I've got enough self-respect to know that much.

Contradicting me, a lock of hair falls over his eye.

"Yeah, no problem. The blanket's in the wash, but I'll leave it in your mailbox sometime today," he says in a raspy response.

A seductive voice, too? Or am I admiring booze-ruined vocal cords? I'm being tested. I must really be stressed out to be turned on by the guy who I thought was half-dead from alcohol poisoning not eight hours ago. This is proof positive being horny fries your brain cells.

I'm suddenly aware I've gone off on a fantasy tangent, and the guy's staring at me.

"Yeah. Great. Sam will be happy," I say. "Hey, what's your name? If we're going to be neighbors, we should at least know each other's names."

I don't get a smile or really any sign of neighborly hospitality.

"It's Parish. I'm sorry, I've got someone on hold. I'll make sure Sam gets his blanket. Goodbye."

And then the door's shut in my face.

For a few seconds I'm not sure what to do, but when I see his outline recede I turn and make my way down the stairs thinking about that awesome name. It's a crying shame this hunk of man is so thoroughly messed up.

"Where's the blanket?" Sam hollers.

"He's going to wash and return it today."

"Good."

Stepping back onto the sand, I throw an arm around his shoulders. He shakes it off. Okay. Rule number two. *Don't touch without asking.* Rule one was, *Don't give his possessions away.*

And that's the end of our conversation. He runs ahead and all the way to the house with me struggling to keep up. Maybe it's our new thing.

This whole dynamic is virgin territory. We've been close ever since he was born. From afar anyway. The fact we were in different states made no difference. Our long-distance conversations and each family gathering I'd fly in for went smoothly for us. When he was little he'd always want to sit next to me. I've prided myself on being the favorite aunt. No matter that I'm his only one.

He was showered with gifts from Auntie Scarlett. Baby clothes to teen favorites. Kids toys, to surfboard. Even trips to Florida's Disney World for the two of us. Living on my own, single and free, gave me disposable income. My travel agent status provided perks I could share with my family. I contributed to his school projects and encouraged his scholastic goals. It was fun. Being childless afforded me the opportunities to spoil him and not worry I was creating a little monster. My sister and Jim watched out for that.

But as I think about all that came before, the reality of what we've been to each other creeps in. To love when you have absolutely no responsibility is an easy kind of affection. And for him to love me back the same. When your only exposure can be measured in hours it's a different animal altogether.

I made no sacrifices. I had no responsibility to make him a good person or calm his fears. I didn't worry if he wasn't doing well in math or feel bad if another kid was mean. Not because I didn't care, but I never knew if or when those things happened. It was good to be blissfully unaware of the minutia of his life. And he only knew the good parts of me. I was fun Aunt Scarlett. That relationship dynamic is a distant cousin to what's starting now.

I didn't choose to be a mother. Never yearned for the experience. But it's chosen me. When my sister told me all those years ago that I was their pick for guardian in case of death, I thought it was an awesome compliment and a remote possibility. I didn't think at all.

By the time I've climbed the wooden stairs leading to our wraparound deck, I'm sweating balls. It's only forty-two degrees and the sun's been hiding behind the fog all morning. Doesn't matter. All the stress put me in a hot flash. Maybe I'm going into premature menopause. Can that happen at thirty-five? Bad start to the day. I vowed it would be our real new beginning after a rocky first night back in the house. A dark mood's beginning to form in my mind. How will we ever make a go of this?

He's left the slider wide open. By the time I get inside, Sam's nowhere to be seen. I follow the path from the great room, past the kitchen, to the hallway. Things look so different. It's not just the pictures that are missing, it's the happy. This used to be a house filled with love and laughter.

Now I just see furniture, meaningless accessories, and walls. There's no sign people actually live here. Tears well up and it's hard to control them. I quickly wipe away the evidence and continue my search.

He's not in his room, the guest rooms, or the office. But down at the end of the hallway comes the sound of stifled crying. Shit. He's in the master.

"Sam?" I give him a warning.

Coming to the open door I knock and peek in, looking for what I already know I'll find. But it's worse. There he sits atop the bed, holding one of the pillows against his face. Kristen's side of the bed shows it's hers. It muffles the sight and sound of crying the body language gives away.

"Oh, Sam," I say, taking a seat next to him.

Tears are streaming down my face too. Fuck rule two. I put an arm around him and pull him close. This time there's no resistance.

An idea passes through my mind. It's going to get me kicked out of the Mother's Guild, but I think the situation calls for something unusual.

"You cry all you want. Meanwhile, Auntie's going to say a bad word, because sometimes it makes me feel better. Just this once. Think you can take it?"

He nods into the pillow.

"Fuck me," I say it quietly. Then louder. "Fuck me."

He lowers the pillow and looks up. Oh. His eyes and snotty nose are red. But he's stopped crying for a moment and he's slightly amused.

"Shall we both say it?" I offer.

He looks surprised at that one. But I get a nod.

"Okay, on three," I say, pointing at him. "One, two, three."

"Fuck me!" we yell in unison.

His voice calls out in anger and sadness. In frustration. But the words have never sounded so innocent. It's poignant. They're followed by a half smile.

"I know I feel better. What about you?" I say.

All I get is a blank look. Feeling better was too much to hope for, but at least he stopped crying.

"Where's all the pictures?" he asks, nostrils flared.

"What pictures?"

"Mom and Dad's. They had them all over the house. Even on the refrigerator. They're gone except for the one in my room."

Oh shit.

"There's none in here anymore. Not one," he says, shaking his head. "And the big jar of sea glass. Dad and I collected them on our walks. Where is everything?"

It doesn't take me long to see he's right and know we've made a mistake. Jim's gone, Kristen's gone, and every stripped shelf and table reflect their absence. It looks like no one has ever lived here. I start talking, spitting out the words in a stream of consciousness.

"It's just that we had your uncles come for a few days and get the house ready for us. I'm sure they meant well. I think they thought maybe you'd be upset seeing so many, um, memories. But everything's in boxes in the garage. Nothing was thrown away. We can look for them when we come back from meeting with your teacher. What do you think?"

Silence. Then a barely there nod. He wipes his nose with his sleeve, takes the pillow with him and walks out of the bedroom.

Scene Break

Turning the black Mercedes SUV I've inherited from Seacliff Court, we drive away from our neighborhood. Sam's middle school's only a few miles from here. I take in the unfamiliar sights.

"There's a lot for me to learn. You're going to have to be my

18

navigator for the first few months, you know," I say, attempting to start a conversation.

"Why are we gonna talk to Mrs. Clark?" he says, ignoring my statement.

"Because I want to introduce myself before you go back to class. There may be things I need to know as your guardian."

"Oh."

"Did you bring the papers I signed? I left them with your backpack."

"Shit. How was I supposed to know? I didn't bring anything," he says angrily.

"We've got to go back. And don't start saying *shit* because I do."

Making an illegal U-turn, I head back. Sam makes an odd sound. It's a huff. A puff of disgust. The kid's schooling me.

"What?" I say, pretending I haven't a clue.

He remains quiet at first, then I see him press his lips together.

"I checked. No one was coming," I add in weak defense.

"That was against the law."

"How do you know?"

"Dad used to say that to my mom when she'd do it."

"Oh. Well, he was right."

"She didn't like to be told either. Like you."

I give him a half smile, but my heart breaks a little. Land mines everywhere. No matter what we do or say.

I'm distracted because up ahead, behind our house, a figure is closing our mailbox. It's that Parish guy returning Sam's blanket.

Holy holly. He's surprisingly fit looking. His biceps look sweet pushing against the long-sleeved runner's shirt. Oh, and the ass. I'd like to pull up a chair and get a ringside seat for that particular show. Pass the popcorn, it's a double feature.

Sam's posture straightens when he realizes his beloved blanket is back. I pull in the driveway and in the process momentarily frighten the man who didn't realize a car was approaching. He looks trapped, subtly turning his head to either side in an attempt at finding the way out. The only thing stopping him is my car blocking the closest exit.

"I'll be right back," I say to Sam.

"Bring the blanket," he orders.

As I open the door and Parish sees me, he rolls his eyes in my direction. *What's his problem?*

Getting out of the car, I approach the cornered rat. He may be stuck here but suddenly those dark chocolate eyes are taking in this new version of me. I'm not sure he'd noticed I'm a woman. The polished meeting-the-teacher look is a hit. There's subtlety to the reading, but no hiding he's checking me out.

"Hi," I say.

"Thanks again for the blanket," he mumbles in my general direction.

I get a half wave as he heads for the front of the car. Oh my God, I think he's trying to squeeze himself between the bumper and the Eucalyptus tree in a desperate attempt at escape.

"Hey, wait!" I say, not really knowing what I'm going to spout next.

The body language is undeniable. His shoulders slump, he stops and turns back to me in defeat. Think he's decided to face the consequences of actually speaking and just get it over with.

"Is it really that painful to talk with me for minute?" I say chuckling.

Then he smiles. Uh oh. That did it.

CHAPTER 3

PARISH

*R*elax. She's not going to bite. Before I can stop myself, a fantasy of her doing that floats through my mind. Doesn't mean anything. Just an automatic response from a guy who's out of practice being in the company of an attractive woman. It's impossible to miss the curve of this one.

Even in the simple skirt and jacket, she looks good. Much better than I gave her credit for this morning. The sexy schoolgirl look with the long hair and bangs. Yep. The boots don't hurt, but I think it's the white blouse that sells the whole package. It's tailored to her and deceptively meant to be conservative.

I was always a sucker for a big boobs/small waist ratio. Didn't realize her chestnut-colored hair was this long and pretty. Nice. And yeah, she has the All-American fresh face thing going on. I used to be drawn to blondes. It's been years since I cared enough to have a type. Unless you include *Women Who Have No Expectations* as a category.

I thought that entire thing out in the time it took her to walk up to me.

"I call a do-over." She holds out her hand. "I'm Scarlett. You're Parish, right? Great name."

Well, now it's required I shake her hand and speak.

"Yes. Nice to meet you," I say with a quick handshake. Hmm. Soft skin. Not sure what I'm afraid of exactly. Other than the horror of being forced to make small talk with the new neighbor.

"I know you must have met Jim and my sister Kristen. They lived here for nine years."

"We haven't met."

Her head tilts and the eyes say, *what kind of asshole am I dealing with?* But she doesn't voice it.

"Are you babysitting for them?" I say. My idea of conversation lacks originality.

What's that look I'm getting? Wait. Why is she speaking in the past tense? Lived? What happened to Happy Family?

"I guess you haven't heard," she says quietly.

Oh no. Her eyes swim with tears. I'm living my nightmare.

"Heard what?" I say.

"They were in an accident. It was fatal."

One fat tear runs down her face. She's biting her lip, but her chin quivers with the painful retelling. She's a pretty crier, but that's not the point. I'm surrounded by tragedy.

"I'm so sorry. How horrible for Sam Boy."

That slips out before I know what I'm saying. But it gets a grin from her. Even though the moment is uncomfortable, I can't help but notice her mouth. *Snap out of it.*

"Is that what you call him? Sam Boy?"

Nodding my head, I try and condense my story. "Sometimes when Sam was little his father would call *Boy* when he wanted him to come in from the beach. Your sister always called him by his name. Because we hadn't met, I just gave all of them the names they'd holler to each other."

"Very creative. What was my sister's name?"

"Babe. That's what her husband called her. She called him *honey.*"

Oh man. The look on her face reminds me of myself when my

Justin's death was new. Whenever someone would talk about memories of him they'd have my undivided attention. From other's perspectives you see a new view of your lost one. A missed piece to the whole.

It's heartbreaking and a particular kind of thrill at the same time. I never wanted them to hold back because it might make me cry.

Her hands lift to her mouth and stop the sob that wants to be set free. My stomach twists in response. I'm not prepared to sooth some else's wounds when my own run so deep.

"Sorry. I shouldn't have told you that. I'm gonna go."

When I begin to turn, she gently places a hand on my arm.

"No. Please. What you told me brings me some joy. Despite evidence to the contrary. It reminds me how much love my sister had in her short life and how happy they were together."

She releases me and wipes her tears with the pads of her fingers.

"I don't know anyone here. Not on this stretch of beach or in town," she says, voice cracking with emotion. "I'm really happy to meet our next door neighbor."

I just nod my head because how can I fight that. Poor woman. It's not going to be easy for her.

"Did you ever actually meet Sam Boy?" she says, gesturing toward the car.

"No. Not really."

Her face brightens. "It would be really great if I could introduce you now. He's having a hard time, as you can imagine. I'd like it if he could at least feel there's a man close by in case we need help in an emergency. I respect your privacy and it's obvious you like to be left alone. I promise not to take advantage."

Like a kid in class who doesn't know the answer, I'm struggling to gather the words and come up with an acceptable response. Usually adept at expressing myself, this surprises me. Suddenly I'm tongue-tied. It gives her the chance to continue.

"And you don't have to worry about Sam bugging you. He doesn't want to talk to anyone. Not even me."

Then she gives me a pleading look I find hard to ignore.

"Yeah, I guess that would be okay," I say with the little enthusiasm I can muster for doing the right thing.

She holds up one finger, gesturing for me to wait while she gets the kid. As she turns and walks back to the car I'm watching that eminently watchable ass. Boom, boom, boom, beat the rim shots in my mind.

When I look up Sam's watching me watching her. I get a hint of a smirk.

The kid's on to me. That deserves a chuckle and a nod. Pretty sharp for a young guy. As he reluctantly gets out I realize it's him I'm doing this for. I recognize the pain behind his eyes. It lives behind mine too.

I just hope neither of them expect too much. I haven't got much to give. If he doesn't want to talk too regularly it should work out. It's most likely the woman I'll have a problem with. Women in general like to talk more than I do. She's stuck in this situation for life now, and it's obvious she's out of her depth. And a little lost too. But she is good to look at.

Guess my readers aren't the only ones who gravitate toward a troubled character. Because like the moon in the day, she's beautifully out of place.

Scene Break

LOUIE'S DINER looks like shit from the outside. The O in the neon sign has gone dark, making it

L UIE's DINER. It doesn't really matter because the parking lot's always full. Regulars like me keep the place in business. Not one of us would think of trading our alliance. Food's great, simple, and fresh. The kitchen's clean. I'm always afraid it's going to be *discovered*.

Why is it residents of beach towns are so territorial? Maybe because like me the people here have found the privacy they need and can't get it in other places. For whatever reason being apart from the crowds and traffic that make up neighborhoods is the pull. In the end we just want to be left alone at the edge of the sea.

The tinkling of the bell sounds as I walk inside. Good, a seat at the counter's open. Too bad the two surfer dudes are on one side. They're talkative, and it's never stimulating conversations. I'm okay on the left. That old guy, with the faded Yankees baseball cap, never says an extra syllable more than what's required.

I make my usual limited eye contact. Then a nod to the cook, Oscar, who can be seen through the passageway to the kitchen. He gives me his normal acknowledgment, a lift of the chin, then goes back to flipping flapjacks.

Terri's on today. She's elevated her waitressing job to an art form. Plus, she reads the room and knows when to stop with the small talk. I take my seat and watch her approach.

"You're late," she says, pouring my coffee. "What've you been up to?"

The one thing I don't like about her are the curved nails. Orange talons that make clicking sounds on the counter like the dinosaurs in *Jurassic Park*.

"I had a few things to take care of."

"You look like hell. Hard night?"

"I'll have the Benedict," I say, closing down further discussion.

"Okay, sugar."

Taking the hint, she walks away and puts in my order. While I'm adding the cream to my coffee, Beavis and Butthead start up.

"Did you see the chick living in the big grey house?" Beavis says, stuffing himself with a forkful of potatoes. Peripherally I see half of it land on the table. His fingers scoop it up and return it to the intended orifice.

"You mean the MILF with the kid?"

My ears perk up.

"No, dude. She's dead. The husband, too. I'm talking about the new chick."

"Dead? When did that happen?"

"They got hit by a drunk driver on 1. Gruesome. It was on the news about a month ago."

"What about the little dude?"

"No. He wasn't with them. The aunt's staying at the house with the kid. A smokin hot chick with big tits."

Idiots. Their conversation pisses me off for multiple reasons.

"How do you know all this?" Butthead says.

"My mom. The chick came into the bank and had all the accounts changed to her name. Dude, she got all the money. Lucky bitch."

What idiots these two are. And obviously the mother at the bank isn't too sharp either. Jesus.

"What about the kid? Doesn't he get any of the inheritance?"

"She's the guardian. Probably will go through it by the time he's old enough to need it."

Thank God the food comes and with it a change of conversation for the geniuses next to me.

Scene Break

The nights usually come slowly. No mystery why. My rule of not drinking till five has made hours move at a snail's pace. It's a miracle I've been able to keep the promise. Don't know if it's going to last but for some reason today hasn't been as bad as yesterday and the thousand days before. It's almost a sign from God. If I was a believer.

I've still got forty-five minutes to get to the drinking hour, and for the first time in a month it seems doable. I might just have a few beers tonight and see how that plan works. It would be good to sleep in my bed.

Got in the three-thousand-word epilogue all in one afternoon session. Early on I discovered I can't write drunk, which helps with my vow. Despite my idol Ernest Hemingway's edict of write drunk, edit sober. He proved it worked for him. He was unusual in that regard. For me both jobs require my being one hundred percent levelheaded.

I stretch out my kinks and close the computer. Moving to the wall of glass, I spot Sam, all alone, making his way toward the shoreline. How he holds his body, the slope of his shoulders, it all tells a story.

I feel for the kid.

Navigating grief is bad enough when you're self-sufficient. When you're young you hardly have any control. Where you live, what you eat, when you get up or go to bed. It's all someone else's decisions. Fuck. Being able to hide myself and control my surroundings so successfully has been my saving grace. Sam, poor kid, can't hide.

I grab my sweatshirt and head out, taking the steps quicker than usual. The sand is cool under my feet and the wind's getting stiffer. I zip up and throw on the hood. Burying my hands in the pockets, I find a couple of sticks of gum. How long have they been there? They're a little stale, but so what. I unwrap one and stick it in my mouth.

"Hey!" I shout over the wind as I approach.

Sam Boy doesn't turn, but just looks over his shoulder at the intruder. Mouth set in a hard line. His private moment gone. There's no smile or wave. Just a look.

"What up?" I say, kicking an empty clam shell over with my toe.

"Nothin."

"You're talking to the waves. That's something."

He gives me a look I recognize, only it's usually coming *from* me. Fuck off it says. I ignore it.

"That's what I do when I don't want to talk to people. I tell the waves my story," I say.

The eye rolling says he thinks I'm a fool. No words needed.

"I do. They hear everything. Especially about the things that hurt."

I stop there. Give him time to take it in. I'm surprised I said that much. But man, the pain on his face. There's no ignoring the fact I see he's alone on the edge of a cliff. And he's just a boy.

When he turns to face me tears are streaming down his cheeks.

"Just let it go, man. It helps. I know from experience."

"What do you have to be sad about?" he says, voice quivering.

I didn't think this out.

"Uh, well I lost someone, too."

"Who?"

"My son."

Shit. Now my eyes are filling up. He sees my reaction and it throws him. He stops crying and watches me.

"Sometimes I'm happy if the only thing I do on any given day is breathe," I sigh.

"I'm sorry," he says, eyes steady on mine.

That was one of the most sincere condolences I've ever heard. Two words offered by a heart so broken there should be no tenderness left.

I find the other piece of gum and hand it to Sam. "Here." I sniff my tears to a stop. "Fuck. Didn't plan on crying."

"Just let it go," he says, giving me a taste of my own medicine.

He takes the gum, and when he looks back up at me he's smiling. You can always count on a kid enjoying a good expletive. I remember my uncle saying the f-word in front of me one time when I was twelve. It was the coolest moment. I felt like an equal.

"Thanks," he says, chewing away. "This might be the best thing I eat tonight."

"What? Why's that?" I say.

"Aunt Scarlett isn't a good cook. She tries, but I don't think she likes having to do it."

I want to laugh, but it's not funny for the kid.

"Then you better learn your way around the kitchen. What's on the menu tonight?"

"She's making a roast with potatoes in the crockpot."

"Well, that sounds pretty good."

He looks at me like I'm crazy. "I don't think she's used one before."

"What makes you say that?"

"When Mom used it, she'd start early in the day. Aunt Scarlett put it on about a half hour ago. And I don't think she used any spices. I looked inside when she was in the other room and it looked bad."

I can't help but chuckle, which makes Sam smile.

"Listen, why don't you come eat with me tonight? We can have pizza and I've got some potato salad. I'll wrap up the leftovers so you can take it home."

He's running the invite around in his mind, probably wondering if I'm a pervert. Or maybe deciding which dinner scenario would be better. Bad food and going to bed hungry, or good food and having to talk at a relative stranger's house.

I put him out of his misery. "You can bring your aunt. She needs to eat too."

His face relaxes. "Okay, I'll ask her. Thanks."

I realize I've left out the most important piece of information.

"Oh, and after dinner I've got to get back to my writing. It's going to be a short night. Is that okay?"

Sam's grin answers my question. No follow up needed. We're already speaking shorthand. He's going to have his favorite meal and be back in his room by seven. As for me, I'll have plenty of time to drink as much or as little as I want before choosing my bed for the night. It's a win-win.

CHAPTER 4

SCARLETT

*W*hat's going on down there? Is that Parish with Sam? I can't tell with that friggin hood hiding the fine face. I hope it's him. Otherwise, some stranger is chatting up a young boy. I've got to be aware. Child predators were never on my radar before. Now they have to be. How will I know if I'm missing some really important thing I should be watching for?

Shit. Where the hell are those binoculars I saw last night? They've got to be close by. Kristen was always a pro at spying on people. She'd take me on her "missions" to watch what her boyfriends were up to. She was in college and I was still in high school and I thought she was the coolest girl I knew. God. So many funny memories. Instead of laughing, they bring tears to my eyes. I miss you, sister.

There those buggers are. I grab the glasses off the hook in the entry to the laundry room then go back to the window.

Oh yeah, that's Parish. The booty. Unmistakable. Then he turns and looks up to his house. Damn. He looks good, face framed by the gray hoodie. *He's a damaged soul* my logical self says. True, but what's my point? We're both damaged. But to invite more misery into an already miserable situation wouldn't be right. I can't expose Sam to that.

It hits me that I'm thinking for two now. It's not just my life that'll be affected by the men I let in. I'm responsible for the moral compass, the physical wellbeing, and the spiritual health of another human being. *Holy shit.* Maybe I should repeat that aloud every morning. Otherwise I could mess this child up, entirely by accident. The realization knots my stomach.

It's the first time I've thought that out. This sucks. *Crying McCryer.* That's me. I wipe the tears from my face and blow my nose on the Kleenex I always have in my pocket lately. Then I go back to watching the two figures at the shore.

Just as the object of my attention starts walking toward his place, the wind picks up. It blows the hood back. Wow, love the dark glasses. Very James Bond. A sigh escapes me with the sight. He's beautiful. It sounds corny but he's really beautiful in a perfect-male way. All the physical attributes line up, but it's something more. And I don't know why I know that. We've barely spoken.

Maybe I'm reading too much into the picture, but despite how many things he's done to push me away I feel he might be tender underneath the hard exterior. And an interesting man hiding behind the lone wolf mask he wears. Or maybe I'm just willing it to be true because he's so hot. Yeah. That's it. Man, he's smokin hot.

My ringtone snaps me out of the dirty fantasy that just began with me sitting on his face. The feel of stubble against my lips. Woo hoo! When I look at the screen I see the intruder's name. Harry. Shit. I legit just lost my lady boner.

"Hello."

"Hi, doll. How's it going?"

I take a seat in the well-worn leather club chair. My bare feet resting on the glass coffee table.

"Shitty. I don't know what I'm doing."

"Oh, it can't be that bad. You're a smart girl. You'll figure it out."

It's that dismissive tone right there that pisses me off. Although, in all honesty, I hadn't noticed it before.

"Uh, no. It's not that kind of thing. My entire life is upside down. I'm not sure you get it," I say dryly.

His sigh confirms my suspicions. He doesn't really give a shit. Otherwise he'd offer some advice or help, or even just the right amount of empathy. Not sure that's in his vocabulary, though. That's what I get for thinking with my genitalia.

"Are you still coming next month?" I say.

There's a short pause preceding his answer. "That's one of the reasons I'm calling. There may be a hiccup in our plans."

"Really?"

"Yeah. I've got this great opportunity I'd hate to pass up. I've been invited on the company ski trip."

My blood pressure begins to rise.

"It's really not so much a ski trip as it is a chance to network for five days. It would be stupid of me to pass it up. I may not get another chance. Not everyone in management is asked, you know."

I have this vision where I'm kicking him in the balls. It's very satisfying.

"Scarlett?"

"I'm here. Yeah, you should definitely go. My family is coming anyway. You'd be bored."

I can almost see the smile on his face.

"Thanks, doll. You're the best."

I used to think that name was so sexy. Now it just sounds like nineteen twenty gangster's lingo.

"I'm about to leave for an appointment. We'll talk later," I lie.

"Okay, great. It was good hearing your voice. I'll call tonight or for sure by tomorrow."

Then he's gone. The fact he's kind of a douchebag is suddenly clear. Whatever. It's not like we were in love. It's just that we had so much fun together traveling whenever we could. My travel agent discounts made it all possible. I thought he'd be a support emotionally. Not that he'd help me, but that he'd listen and respond with compassion.

But he was mostly a decent fuck buddy if I'm being honest. I guess that was all I was to him. Oh yeah, and a cheaper way to travel. So who am I mad at? Turning to the mirror hanging by the entry to the kitchen, I realize who's at fault. Oh yeah. Me.

Better check how our dinner's coming. Funny, I don't smell anything. I get up and move to the kitchen, glancing to make sure Sam's still visible. When I lift the lid of the crockpot I get an unfortunate surprise. It doesn't look like it's cooked at all. The raw hunk of meat sits under two dense uncooked whole potatoes. *What the hell?* I feel for the heat on the outside. It's on. This cooking thing sucks the big one. No wonder I never liked it.

Are there fast food places nearby? Do they have Dine and Dash out here, or Uber Eats? I go to the refrigerator and peruse the shelves. Jim's cousin and his wife stocked it for us and the pantry as well. But that was four days ago. Most things here must be non-perishable. My bad. I thought going to the grocery store with Sam would be bonding. Hasn't happened yet.

There's eggs. I could do that much. Scramble a few of those. What goes with it? Do I make breakfast for dinner, or is that wrong for a kid? Shit. Shit. Shit. I know nothing about any of this. Here's some green olives. What if I chop those up and put them in the eggs? Is there cheese? Oh yeah, the drawers. Eureka! Okay. I'm making an olive and cheese scramble and toast. Pretty creative if I don't say so myself. It's the best I can do tonight. Tomorrow I'll try again.

The sound of the slider opening pulls my attention.

"Sam?"

He walks into the kitchen and finds me in the refrigerator.

"Hey."

Putting on my best happy face, I give him the news. "New plan for dinner. That roast isn't working out."

He gets this pissy look on his face, as if I'm a moron.

"You should have started in the morning. It takes hours," he says like it's information everyone should know.

An arm comes around me and grabs a Coke.

"Why didn't you tell me that? And are you supposed to drink that many Cokes in one day? That's your third," I say.

"I thought you knew what you were doing. And yeah. I can have all I want."

"I'm pretty sure that's not true. Your mother wouldn't let you do that."

The look I'm getting could freeze a lava flow. He leaves the Coke on the counter and walks out.

"We're having pizza at Parish's at six." The voice trails behind him.

See, now I don't know what to do. I don't like the idea of a kid barking orders, but I already reprimanded him about the soft drink. How many issues can I address at the same time?

Okay, Scarlett. You won the Coke battle for now. Let him claim a victory on the dinner plans. And would being within close proximity to Parish be so bad? My mom tells me it's about compromise with kids. She says you pick your battles.

Scene Break

"Why are you bringing the nuts?" Sam says with a confused expression.

We climb the stairs to Parish's front door. I see him in the background through the dark glass. This time he's wearing pants. There's not a cigarette butt to be seen on the deck.

"When you go to someone's home for a meal you bring a little gift."

The door opens, and I'm taken aback. Drool may be involved. He looks less like a man recovering from a drunken night on the beach and more like a model in an ad for *Guys You*

Want to Fuck magazine. Hadn't noticed the salt and pepper temples.

The white soft-looking top highlights his jet-colored hair. Then there's what's going on below. God. He wears charcoal running pants and they hang low on his hips. The waistband shows through the shirt. And one other thing. #restingbulge. It's impossible to miss the most important detail.

"Nuts?" I say, offering my gift.

A chuckle leaves his mouth and I get a grin. He's probably used to the effect he has on women.

"Come in. I put the pizza in when I saw you two coming."

We walk into the spider's lair and my eyes scan the room and take in the details. Women are so good at that. Before deciding where to sit, I've noticed all the books. There's so many they take up three walls, floor to ceiling. The spines are worn. These aren't for show. He's a voracious reader. On the desk sits a laptop and a thick notepad. Everything here seems ordered. The man's neat. Interesting.

"Take a seat. I'm finishing the salad," he says, gesturing to the barstools at the counter where he stands chopping a tomato.

Sam is looking around like I'd like to. Up close to the shelves and peeking around the corners.

"Does that bother you?" I say to Parish, nodding toward Sam who's unaware there's two other people in the room.

"No. Let him look. I'm an open book." He pauses. "A short story."

"I think you're more of an unread novel in a foreign language."

He stops chopping and looks at me. It's piercing.

"Why do you say that?"

"Because I can't make sense of you. But I think there's lots to the tale."

His brows draw together but the grin remains.

"Hey, did you write this?" Sam calls from across the room.

We both turn to see him taking a book from the shelves. I can't see the text from here, but I take it the author's first name is Parish.

"You wrote all these?" Sam asks.

"Yeah. That's what I do."

"How come there's no picture of you?" Sam says.

"I didn't want that. Are you a reader, Sam?"

"No. Just what I have to at school. What're your books about?"

"I write about a detective. He lives at the beach like we do. In fact, it's this beach I'm describing."

"Maybe I can read one of them."

Parish tilts his head. "They might be a little mature for your age group. But I think you could take it. You'd have to get your aunt's permission."

Sam looks at me and the message is clear. He wants my permission.

"We can talk about it," I say.

"If not, I can suggest a book for you. I know some really good ones," Parish adds.

This is an interesting development. A writer? Didn't see that one coming. But I should have. The tortured artist syndrome is pretty clichéd. When he looks at me I give him a raised eyebrow and a nod of approval. I'll be ordering a book on Amazon tonight. I'm interested in mature writing.

"Okay, I'm pretty casual here. Want to eat on the couch? I don't have an actual dining table."

"Yes!" Sam's reaction is immediate. That's the lightest expression he's worn in a month.

Soft Break

"That was the best pizza I've ever had," Sam says, licking the cheese from his finger.

"Thanks, man. When you live alone learning to cook is a must. Otherwise you starve."

That's the first time I've heard him laugh since the accident. There's no doubt he's connecting to Parish. And from what I've seen here, it might be a good thing. Other than occasionally being the drunk passed out on the beach, he's surprisingly together. Or at least he can play together-guy.

"So, Scarlett. What about your story? You have a boyfriend?"

"No. No boyfriend," I say, completely surprised by the question.

"What about Harry?" Sam pipes in.

This is one of those times I heard my sister talk about. When your kid contradicts you by telling the unvarnished truth. She'd say it was always mortifying. *Kristen, I hear you. I get it now.*

"Who's Harry?" Parish directs his question to the boy.

"He's a guy that Aunt Scarlett brings to holidays. And they go on trips together."

"You like him, Sam?"

"Not really," he says. "He's too into himself."

Parish laughs with that one.

"Well, let's not tell all my secrets," I say, shooting Sam a death ray.

For some reason both Sam and Parish think the whole thing's funny.

"He's just a friend who comes with me sometimes," I add.

"Dad said you were boyfriend girlfriend because you stayed in the same room together."

I give my nephew a shut-the-fuck-up look which hits its mark.

"I'm gonna take a walk on the beach," Sam says.

"Want company?" I offer.

He walks to the door without turning around. "No."

"Come back before it gets dark," I say.

And he's gone.

"Sometimes a guy just needs to be alone," Parish says in response to my worried expression. "You can watch him from here."

I sigh my agreement. "Let me help with the cleanup," I add, trying to fill the space between us with words.

He doesn't move. Just stretches his arm over the back of the couch and watches me across the room. His legs are spread and he looks like he's very comfortable. I'm sitting in the comfy chair but that's a deceptive description. His silence is making me feel awkward. Too self-aware. But being the observer suits him.

"No. I'll do it later. Relax."

Relax? *Oh yeah, that's going to happen.* My mind shuffles through the conversation starters I have in my arsenal.

"So, tell me about you," I say, instantly regretting my unoriginal question.

"There's not much to tell. I've lived here for five years. I write. I walk on the beach. I drink. That's about it."

Now what am I supposed to do with that?

"I think you may be giving me the condensed version. No one gets to our age without some dramatic chapters," I say.

He tilts his head and smiles. "Our age? How old are you?"

"Thirty-five. And a half," I giggle. "Those halves used to be so important to me. Somewhere along the way I stopped wanting to quicken the process."

"You look younger. I'm forty-three. And I don't mind the passing of time. In fact, I wish the whole thing would speed up."

"Why in the world would you wish that? Looking forward to senior discounts?" I tease.

He shakes his head. "No. It's just all too much sometimes."

"Too much what?"

He abruptly stands and looks out the window. "I don't know what I'm talking about. Forget what I said. I'm gonna grab a beer. Want one?"

I'm not going to forget. I want to find out what burden he's carrying. Because that's what just showed on his face. But this isn't the right time.

"No. Not tonight," I say. "But I will have another piece of pizza."

He likes that.

"Good. That's the best review a cook can get."

Moving to the kitchen, he gets our second helpings.

"What about you, Scarlett? Tell me about your life before you came here."

He makes my plate with a fresh pizza slice and another one of the sweet pickles I took two of earlier.

I see him guzzle a few swallows of the beer before returning.

"My life was…well, it was pretty great. I'm from Montana and until last month I planned on staying. My whole big crazy family's there. My parents and three brothers. Kristen was the only one who moved."

"Big family."

"Thank God. My brothers have really rallied around us. They call every day to see if Sam and I are okay. They're all mindful of how difficult it is for their nephew. And they always try to make us laugh."

"Why did your sister move to this isolated beach?"

"Jim was from here. His family owns lots of property in town."

"Are you the eldest?"

"I'm the baby. My father says I was the big surprise. They thought they were done with babies when I showed up."

"Three big brothers. I bet your boyfriends had it tough."

I chuckle at the memories. "Well, they tried to interfere all they could. But I had a mind of my own. Even at sixteen."

"Somehow that doesn't surprise me. What kind of work do you do?"

"I'm a travel agent so really I can work from anywhere. But it's a moot point now."

"Why's that?"

"I'm taking a year off to be here. We all decided moving Sam would be too much for him right now. I'm going to try to get him through middle school in this familiar setting. He'll graduate from eighth grade next year. I'm hoping to get back to Montana then," I say, pausing for a few beats.

"We're all going to decide together what works for high school. My family is awesome, and they're helping Sam and I get through this. I can't imagine doing it on our own. Bottom line, this isn't a part-time job."

"Sounds overwhelming for someone who got dropped into it."

"It is. Even with the support. Completely overwhelming. I'm not sure what to make for dinner, let alone how to parent. Sam's a good kid. I love him with all my heart. But he didn't plan on having me as his mother, and I didn't plan on being one. God. That sounds terrible," my voice trails off.

Parish scoots to the edge of the couch and rests his elbows on his knees. "I think you're allowed to have doubts. From what I can see you might make a good mom. I've been around someone who wasn't meant for motherhood. It doesn't look anything like this."

Interesting.

"Thank you for saying that."

"You're underestimating what a compassionate thing you're doing. For your nephew, your sister, her husband. You're voluntarily giving up whatever it was you dreamed your life would be. I think it's remarkable."

The tears come without my permission. My chin is quivering. And all because a virtual stranger saw how difficult my journey is and he showed empathy. I wipe the drops from my cheeks and try getting ahold of myself.

"Sorry. That's the second time today I've cried in front of you. Usually my girlfriends are the ones I go to. But a telephone conversation just isn't the same as a shoulder."

He gets up and comes close, sitting on the edge of the coffee table. Our knees touching, he takes my hands in his. A shiver runs down my spine.

"You can't rely on me to be there every time, because no kidding I'm fucked up on a regular basis. But if you have a bad day you're welcome to see if I'm having a good one. If I am, you can use my shoulder. Same goes for Sam."

I squeeze his warm strong hands. My voice is silenced by the lump in my throat and the big emotion causing it.

"I'm short on friends here too," he says. "My problem is I'm way too fucking picky. You and Sam are the first people I've been able to tolerate in years."

He chuckles when he says it, but I think there's truth hidden between the words.

"Being tolerated is the first thing I look for in a friend. Yeah, I think we can do that," I say.

CHAPTER 5

PARISH

*S*o far so good. The morning after that first dinner I was afraid I'd made a rookie mistake. Lowering my wall enough to let Sam and Scarlett over it was impulsive. But three weeks ago, as October turned into November, I began to relax into the idea. It's not so bad waving to my neighbors or joining Sam for an occasional walk to the lighthouse or coves. It's freeing not to have to avoid the people next door.

And even if the only good thing to come of it is that I haven't slept on the beach since that night, or gotten stinking drunk, it's enough. Baby steps.

The last time I was around a thirteen-year-old boy was when I was thirteen. My Justin would have been that age. Boys are almost everything at thirteen. Almost men, almost tall, almost driving, and almost ready for their first kiss and the life changing realization of what it will lead to.

Sam's at the doorstep to it all. If he can get through the sorrow, he's about to be in a great stage of life where it's all about first times. You have no idea yet what all the firsts feel like, you just know everyone loves remembering theirs. Anticipation is at its height. Life still promises.

Mostly the two of them leave me alone. I've a sense Sam told Scarlett about my loss. A tenderness crept between us that only could have come from sympathy. She knows.

And they respect the fact I need to be holed up in my writer's cave every day. When we do get together I value the break. All three of us have eased into the friendship. It's taken almost seven weeks. Not one of us rushed the connection.

When we do hang out it's easy, nothing's forced. I like listening to them talk. Sam and I haven't had any additional discussions about his sadness or any reference to his parents' accident. I'm letting him take the lead on that one. Sometimes when you're forced to put words to grief it feels too fucking painful. Other times it's cathartic. The problem is you never know which it's going to be.

But we talk about everything else. The kid has opinions. He makes me laugh and get out of my own head. Now that I'm thinking of it, who's soothing who?

I find myself drinking less and I guess that's because some of my tragic thoughts have been tempered. I'm distracted. Sometimes a whole hour goes by without me thinking of that horrible day. That's new.

I still have alcohol every night, but the passed-out drunk is taking a break. Lately, if I have too much I put myself to bed. In the house. The smokes have lost their draw altogether. I was never really into it anyway. It enabled the drinking. Cigarettes and whiskey just went together so smoothly. I'm sure I smelled like an ashtray. It seems disgusting now.

Scarlett's an interesting woman. I haven't taken the time to find out if a woman's interesting or not in a long time. Forgot how satisfying a good conversation can be. The kind you get lost in. All of a sudden three hours have passed. Those are the kind Scarlett and I have. Sometimes it's on the phone and other times it's while we walk the beach.

In another world I'd be looking for more from her. God

knows I've noticed all the details. The eyes. Those are hard to get past. In bright sunlight they look greenish, but when we're on the deck, under the lowlight of the lantern, they change to a blue. That along with the chestnut-colored hair makes an impression.

Then there's the mouth. I've imagined all sorts of scenarios. Simply put, I like to look at it. The full bottom lip and the defined bow on top make for a beautiful combo. Lipstick's redundant because her natural shade is pink. Kissing them could end some man's search.

To say I like what I've seen of her body is an understatement. Once in a while I catch myself looking at her breasts a little too long. Like teenage boys do when they haven't yet actually touched one. I can't help myself. Another adolescent excuse. Maybe she leans over or jogs in the sand, whatever. My eyes automatically dart to those two beautiful orbs and the pink nipples I've imagined in every masturbation session I've had since we met. They're my kryptonite.

And below those gifts a narrow waist curves in and out to rounded hips. Turn around, baby. That thought comes into my mind on a daily basis. Looking at her ass is becoming habit. Solid and high. That's all a man can hope for, and she's delivered.

What the fuck, Parish? I return to reality and call her cell. She picks up on the fourth ring, just as I was about to disconnect.

"Hi," she says breathing heavy.

"Am I interrupting something?"

She starts giggling. I don't hate the sound.

"Unfortunately, no. I was exercising to that yoga DVD I told you I found."

"I'm pretty sure it's not supposed to be aerobic. Are you certain you're doing it right?"

"No I'm not! I told you I'm a klutz. I hate it anyway. Thanks for interrupting my downward dog."

I'd like to go downward dog on her right now.

"Why are you exercising in your house when you have the greatest natural treadmill right outside?"

"What are you suggesting?" she says.

"Interested in a walk?"

There's no hesitation. "Sure."

"Grab your coat. It's chilly."

"Are you kidding? I'm sweating here!"

She can't see my smile or know how good it feels just to realize I'm going to see her in a minute.

"Meet you outside," I say.

Before I leave, I run my hands through my hair and check my breath. This is the house of one mirror, and it's in the bathroom. I consider it for just a moment. I'm good. She might be waiting.

At the last moment I grab a handful of the butterscotch candies in the glass bowl and stuff them in the pocket of my sweatshirt. They've become a habit as I leave behind other more destructive ones.

The wind blows my hair in every direction as I close the door behind me. The immense energy of the ocean is putting on a show. But the bright sunlight accompanies it. The perfect day. Like a dog in the wind, I'm feeling frisky.

Making it to the bottom of the stairs I turn to see she's walking my way. No ponytail today. The hair is loose and dancing in the breeze. It looks beautiful. The white v-neck long sleeved T-shirt and black yoga pants make me grin. They don't hide the shape of her.

I wait and watch as she approaches. At first she waves and meets my gaze. But when I don't look away her behavior changes. Her head dips and she looks down at her feet as she marches forward. All the while there's a smile she's holding back by biting her lip. She's embarrassed by my stare. I like the reaction. A lot.

When she gets within a few yards she picks up a rock and throws it at me.

"Hey! Don't start something you can't finish, woman," I say, dodging the stone.

She laughs and hits my arm as she passes. I jog the two steps to catch up.

"You started it," she says as we walk.

I don't deny the charge. We both know I was enjoying the view. I've got a feeling it's about to get better. As she passed me I noticed how cold she was getting already. It's a nipple extravaganza. I'm so glad she ignored my coat suggestion. Thank you, God. Maybe you're there after all.

"You cold by any chance, Scarlett?" I say with a raised eyebrow and a meaningful tone.

"No, it feels good," she says with no conviction. Then she laughs.

The sound of that was in my dream the other night.

"That's bullshit. Your teeth are chattering," I say, jogging a few steps ahead.

I turn and walk backwards in front of her.

"Then there's *this* whole thing happening." My hands making concentric circles in front of her T-shirt.

The look on her face is priceless. Shock followed by amusement. She crosses her arms over her breasts.

"What a pervert you are!"

"True," I say, taking off my zip up. "Here, before those things tear holes in your shirt."

She doesn't fight me. I help her into it as we walk to the edge of the ocean. It looks like she's wearing a giant's sweatshirt. It's cute on her. *Down, boy.*

"Hey! Look!" she says, pulling a butterscotch from the pocket and tossing it to me.

"I put them there for us."

"Nice."

She unwraps one for herself and I watch surreptitiously as she sucks on the hard candy. My superhero peripheral vision is coming in handy. Oh, brother. My dick's waking up. Maybe I should pour butterscotch syrup over my penis when we get back and see what happens. That image isn't helping the situation. *Look away, man.*

"Sam said you showed him some coves. Is that where we're headed?" she says.

"No. They're in the opposite direction."

We walk silently for a while, just sucking on our butterscotch candy and enjoying the beautiful day. She plays in the foam of the waves that roll to the shore. The impromptu dance makes me grin. And when she sees my reaction she smiles too.

"I needed this. Thanks," she says, resuming her walk.

"Having a bad day?"

"It's just that every time I think I'm making some progress with Sam, I crash and burn. Today was the worst. It's pretty demoralizing."

"What happened?"

"He's going through puberty. You remember how bad that can be."

"Oh yeah. Confusing, embarrassing."

"Exactly. Well, I only know about girls because my brothers had already gone through it by the time it was my turn. My perspective is from that angle. This morning before school I made a *huge* mistake," she says, emphasizing the word huge.

"What did you do? I want to hear this one."

She stops walking and I follow suit. Her eyes squeeze shut and her face scrunches up.

"I walked in on him masturbating." A squeal comes out as she relives the event.

I start laughing. "What the hell, Scarlett?"

Another hit to my bicep.

"Stop it. It's not funny! I didn't do it on purpose. I thought he'd overslept, and I just walked in. There he was with a sock on his ...and he was looking at his phone propped up on a pillow ...

and I got embarrassed and ran into the door as I was leaving! Look."

She unzips the sweatshirt and peels down the shoulder of her T. A raised black and blue bruise marks the spot.

I'm laughing so hard I'm doubled over with my hands on my knees.

"It's not funny! You asshole!"

"I'm the asshole? I'm pretty sure you're the voyeur in this story."

"What?!" Her voice goes up three octaves.

Then in response to the accusation, she shoves me over. Like the Hulk. The unexpected move sends me onto the wet sand, where the reach of an icy wave rolls over me, shocking my senses. When I sit upright and make eye contact, a hand goes to her mouth.

"That's gonna cost you, princess." I spit out a mouthful of seawater.

It's on. She screams and turns to run. I'm too quick for her and grab her ankle as she tries escaping.

"Wait! I'm sorry I did that to you!" she yells.

"Too bad, baby."

I take her down, roll her over and pin her arms in the sand under the last of the retreating wave. When she tries using her legs to wiggle free, I lay on top of her. Our clothes are drenched and stuck to our skin. Feeling the softness of her breasts and the erectness of the nipples makes my dick push hard against her squirming body. It's turning out to be one hell of a day.

Leaning close so she can hear me over the sound of the waves, I give my warning.

"You're about to get *really* wet."

Her lifted eyebrows tell me she's a little shocked. The misinterpretation is exactly what I hoped for. That's the precise moment the next wave rolls over us both. Uh oh, that was bigger than expected. It rolls me off her, then with its retreat tries to pull us out to sea.

My hands reach for hers. Pulling myself upright I lift her in one quick move. Neither of us are speaking, but all kind of messages are being exchanged silently. Scarlett's getting a kick out of this. My smile's genuine. I move a long strand of wet hair from her lips.

"The ocean looks good on you," I say.

We're both freezing. Doesn't matter. I take her face in my hands and eliminate the space between us. She presses against me and gazes into my eyes. God. She's so beautiful. And my dick. It's pushing back. Water drips from our hair and eyelashes, from her perfect mouth.

Fuck waiting. I lean in, and with one hand wrapped around her neck and fingers threaded through her wet hair, I take the kiss. Slender arms lock around my waist. The sea's wild and the wind is whipping the foam to free floating peeks that break off and float in the air.

We're trying to keep our balance, feet sinking as the tide ebbs and flows. But this kiss. Neither feels the need to cut it short. Nothing's held back. The feeling coursing through me is fucking unbelievable. Electric. Lips part and our eyes lock.

"Well, that happened," Scarlett says.

"I'm not sorry it did. You?"

"Not really."

We start laughing. I grab her hand and lead us to solid ground. All the way, random butterscotch candies dot the shore or float in the shallows.

"Was it my wrestling skills that turned you on?" she says, twisting out the water from her sweatshirt's hem.

"It was your mouth," I say, sure of the answer.

She likes that, I can tell by the way she's biting her bottom lip.

"What about the friend thing?" she says. "Are we just going to conveniently ignore that?"

"Can't we do both?"

Her expression hides what she's thinking. I'm not certain she agrees this is a good idea.

I wrap my arms around her shivering body and lean my nose against hers. "I don't think it would be so bad to enjoy what we both want. In fact, I'm feeling very friendly. We could go back to my place and get warm."

But the suggestion falls flat. She gently pushes me away, and something new shows up on her face. I think it's determination of some kind, and not in my favor.

"Let's not ruin what we have, Parish. As much as I enjoyed that awesome kiss, I'm freezing. Let's go back."

What? Didn't see that coming. Where did I go off course? She starts walking back. Fuck me. Now that I've kissed her I want more.

"Wait," I say, catching up. "Let's think this out. What's the harm of enjoying a kiss, or ten? We're adults and capable of not letting it ruin our relationship."

Scarlett stops walking and looks me squarely in the eyes.

"See how fast this escalated? It was just a little kiss. Now you're talking ten and getting warm and going back to your place."

"Little kiss? Are you really going with that?"

I get a grin. "That may not be completely accurate."

I nod my head in agreement but let her know I'm questioning her assessment.

"What?" she says softly.

"It was good and you know it. Why should we deny ourselves a little tenderness? Some physical mercy. We both could use it."

Her hand lifts to my face.

"That all went through my mind. Before you said it I was saying it to myself."

I'm unfamiliar with having to talk a woman into kissing me. It feels odd. But in this case I'm not above begging.

She starts walking.

THE BEACH IN WINTER

"What's the problem then? Tell me, Scarlett."

"Something horrible has happened."

I take her by the shoulders and turn her to face me. "What?"

"I've started to think like a parent. Like a mother. It sucks."

"So? Mothers kiss. And more."

She gives me a reluctant grin and a meaningful stare. "You have no idea how much I want to kiss you again. It shocks me as much as it does you that we're not heading to your bed right now."

"Sounds great to me."

"But this whole selfless thing is happening without me consciously trying. I'm starting to put Sam first. Now that sounds kind of beautiful in theory. And surprisingly unselfish. But in practice, like I said, it sucks the big…"

I interrupt her soliloquy by wrapping my arm around her waist and pulling her close. My lips find hers. There's no resistance despite the things she just said. It's me who pauses for the question that just occurred to me.

"How is not kissing me putting Sam first?"

She looks up into my eyes. "He can't lose you as his friend right now. I won't risk having that happening. Because his life's a shitstorm and you're one of the few things that make it better. That's more important than our sexual satisfaction."

It's noble. I've got to give her that. It's right. Morally right. Compassionate. But the most important thing I'm taking from the conversation are the words *sexual satisfaction.* I'm encouraged she's thinking ahead.

CHAPTER 6

SCARLETT

I'm screwed. Three days after our wrestling match in the waves and it's all I can think about. He's stayed away, damn him. My stand in the sand was a bit too firm and obviously taken seriously. It might be a good thing. I'm not sure my will would be strong enough to hold steady. A little distance will be to my benefit.

Sam has been to Parish's house and yesterday after school they took a walk to check out the lighthouse and talk with the light-house keeper. I wasn't invited.

There's so much I have to do to get ready for Thanksgiving, and I only have five days to get it done. Grocery shopping, house cleaning, and making sure to put a few decorations up. I have a few new ones waiting. I can't put up Sam's familiar holiday decorations.

Thank God the family's coming for the weekend. I can only imagine the meal I'd be capable of making without their help. It'll be great having my support system here and laughing together like we always do.

I just want to take a breath. It's exhausting.

Seems like every waking moment requires one hundred

percent of me. I'm required to learn new things, find right answers, be a chauffeur and bodyguard. There's nothing left over for my own life. I respect mothers on a whole other level now. I didn't realize what it takes.

I haven't begun to know the depth and breadth of the position or what it takes from a woman over a lifetime. Or what it gives. I only know for me it's composed of great joy and soul-sucking frustration. I guess nothing will be the same anymore.

A loud knock on the slider glass scares the shit out of me. My hand goes to my heart. Then I see who it is and that heart starts racing.

"Morning," Parish calls.

I'm not completely dressed, still in nightshirt and my favorite Uggs. My weekend uniform till I'm forced to dress and get my shit together. The hair is wild and unkempt. Sleeping in has gone by the wayside like most other habits I enjoyed as a single woman.

"Morning," I say, sliding the door open. "You scared me!"

I didn't factor in what my appearance would do to him. He looks me up and down with a straight face. His jaw tenses. Then I get a big smile.

"Well Scarlett, I see you're not wearing pants. Is that how you answer the door?"

"How do you know if I'm wearing pants or not? Maybe you just can't see them. And how I answer the door is none of your business. I seem to recall you were pant-less the first time we met, and I never mentioned it."

"Touché."

A delicious look comes over his face, mirroring mine. We're amusing the shit out of each other. Trouble.

"So, where's Sam? Did he go to the game?" he says.

"What game? He said he was going to his friend's house a few blocks away."

He walks inside and takes a seat on the couch. Fingers thread behind his head as he stretches his legs out.

"Not sure that's a hundred percent accurate."

"Why are you saying that?"

"Because he told me there was a football game at the school today. You know he used to play, right?"

"I knew he played last year. But he never mentioned anything about wanting to get involved this year. Shit."

"Get dressed. Let's go see if he's there."

"You're very bossy today."

He looks at me with mischief in his chocolate eyes. "Don't you like it just a little?" he says softly.

He's one hundred percent serious.

"Maybe," I answer.

So am I.

Scene Break

It seems like we've been walking for a mile.

"There they are," Parish says, pointing to the team on the far side of the field.

"You sure? There's another team playing over there." I motion to the big crowd gathered to the right.

"No. That's Sam's school colors. They show up at my door every year selling candy to raise money for the team."

"And you answer it? That's a surprise."

"I've got a soft spot for the kids. It's the adults I try to avoid."

"Someday I want to hear why that is. Do you think you could let me in that far?"

He considers the question for more than a few beats. I don't press.

"Yeah. But this isn't the place. Okay?"

I just nod, afraid he'll change his mind if I respond at all.

We walk the rest of the way in silence until we're close enough to see the faces.

"Look. There's Sam. He's playing," I say.

Parish checks out the scene, then with a hand at my back, leads me into the second row seats at the end of the makeshift bleachers. The blonde woman sitting behind us is watching his every move. Whore. I almost start laughing at my silent overreaction.

"I'm a little hurt. Why didn't Sam want me to come?"

He leans in so our conversation stays private. "He just wants to be invisible right now."

I take the whole thing in and roll it around. I get it.

"I thought if we came together we'd be less likely to stand out," he says. "Nobody knows we're here for him."

I look in his dark chocolate eyes and my heart melts. It's easy to see the good man he is. It's been hidden behind something I haven't identified yet.

"Thank you for being so kind to Sam. He's just a kid who feels alone and afraid."

He places a hand in mine and squeezes. Are those tears I see welling?

"He sees us," Parish says, breaking eye contact. Taking his hand away he returns it to his sweatshirt pocket.

When I look, Sam's eyes are on us. It's not happiness or anger I see. He's taking in the scene and processing.

"Don't wave," Parish says.

"I'm wasn't going to," I lie. "I just hope he doesn't get pissed and walk off because we're here."

But he doesn't. For the rest of the game we cheer and encourage all the players, careful not to single Sam out. For his part he allows our presence and continues playing to the last quarter. That's when we decide to bug out. We can't give our identities away before he's ready to claim us.

All the way back to his car we're each lost in deep thought. I'm betting it's about the same thing though. Parish's story needs to be told and heard. Opening the car door for me, I slide in. When he comes around and takes the driver's seat there's a look of sadness on his face.

"It's chilly," he says, rubbing his hands together.

Leaning his head back he closes his eyes. It's obvious he's

stalling. Whatever it is that wounds him so deeply is hard to put words to.

He makes no moves to start the engine, but instead angles his body toward mine and looks into my eyes. I'm holding my breath in anticipation.

"So you really want to know what happened to ruin a man?" he says.

How do I answer that?

A big sigh escapes his lips and a new expression dresses his face. Wow. Whatever he's about to tell me is so painful it steals the light in his eyes.

"I think Sam told you I had lost my child. He asked why I was sad and that's as much as I told him."

I just nod.

"What I didn't say, what I wouldn't say was that it was a school shooting. The shooter used an assault rifle on the children."

Tears run down his face and he can't wipe them away fast enough.

"Justin was shot four times and died on the floor of his second-grade class. Along with six other children, their teacher, and a teacher's aide."

Has a voice ever sounded so broken, or filled with anguish? I feel like the earth just stopped rotating. Oh my God. My God. And then the tears start falling. There's no stopping them for either of us.

It's hard to know what to say or how to say it. Just hearing the facts is crushing. To live with it must be unbearable. How does a parent survive being so brutally broken? How do the images ever leave their mind?

"Oh, Parish. How horrible. Come here. Please let me hold you."

Taking him in my arms I sense the emotional pain and suffering emanating from his body. He buries his head in the crux of my neck, and his body collapses into my embrace. This is grief at its rawest.

56

Like a mother kisses her child, I hold him. Stroking his hair and kissing his head with pure tenderness. Wanting to make it better. But knowing there's nothing and no one who can do that. I try to get as close as I can.

I ache to say the perfect thing. Something that will ease his pain if even for one second. But without a doubt know it's an impossibility. So, I stay quiet. Except for the crying. It's not a choice, but an involuntary response to the most horrific thing I've ever been told.

Now I understand the drinking and the smoking and how being unconscious on the beach was infinitely better than being awake.

Scene Break

We drove home in blessed quiet. Not that it was uncomfortable. I think we both were letting our psyches rest in the aftermath of the conversation. As soon as I got home I knew what I had to do. So I'm channeling detective Kristen, armed with my laptop. My cell is within reach and I've got a soft blanket covering my legs. I'm going to find whatever I can about Parish's son and the shooting. Although I don't even know where it happened.

But it's kind of surprising. As I Google *Parish Adams,* it's site after site about his novels and barely anything pertaining to his personal information. And absolutely nothing about a child.

Parish Adams may be a nom de plume. Okay, let me go after this another way. I dig for school shootings. It takes barely five minutes for me to find it. Here it is. I think. A newspaper article from *The Daily Breeze. Redondo Beach School Massacre.* The year matches what Parish said. I look for the victims list and my eyes go right to the second name, Justin Adams, age eight.

A deep sigh slips out as I look at the innocent faces who lost their lives. He was a beautiful blond boy with a cherub-like smile. Then I see the other picture. It's Parish at his child's funeral, his face contorted in grief. I start crying. Again.

Underneath the photo the journalist's words grab my attention.

New York Times best-selling author, P.J. Adams attends his child's funeral.

What?

He's P.J. Adams?

I'd read both of his novels before never seeing one again. I always looked for his next one, but it never came. Oh my God. He's been hiding behind his full name. And he's changed genres. Stayed in fiction but went to a detective series.

Unbelievable. I'm going to have to hold this information close, till he's ready to discuss it. It may be never. In the meantime I'm going to read everything he's written, including the first two again as his real self.

Scene Break

Parish hasn't left his house for three days. I've walked to these windows and slider a hundred times. Watching for him. Yesterday I just sat in the sand in front of his steps hoping he'd feel bad for me having to do that. But I got nothing.

Even Sam's disturbed by Parish's absence on the beach. It's nearly winter and the season reflects my inner reality. I'm cold with thoughts of his suffering and I feel life's chill stronger than ever before.

Why are we all destined to bear so much? What purpose does crippling sadness have? Why isn't he calling?

Sam will be home at three thirty. There's time. I'm going over there and knock on his door till he lets me in. I grab my jacket and head out.

With every step across the sand I'm having an imaginary conversation with him. What I'm going to say, what he's going to respond with. How I'll make it better for him, if just for today. But first he has to open the door.

I take the stairs boldly so he can hear me coming. When I get to the deck I wait. I can't see him through the glass. But I ring the bell anyway.

Is that him on the couch? Was that the top of his head moving with the sound of the doorbell? But then nothing. I start knocking and pretend I know for certain he's there.

"Parish! Open up!"

Silence.

"Parish, god dammit, open the fucking door!!"

At first there's no sign of life. Then very slowly a head rises from behind the couch and turns toward me. Yes!

"Come on. Just let me in for five minutes. You better do it. I'm not fooling around," I yell, trying to sound threatening.

I watch as he makes his way to the door, pausing before he decides to do as asked. As I demand.

I'm reminded of that first day, when just his bloodshot eye peeked out. But today, as the door opens the required two inches, they're clear. He looks tired but not hungover. The rest of him looks the same, hair in his eyes, stubble, a serious expression.

"Scarlett."

That's all he says. Just my name.

"Parish. Are you alright?"

"Not sure that's possible. But I'm trying."

"You don't look like you're getting much sleep."

"It's overrated."

My heart breaks for his struggle. "Can I come in?"

For a few beats he's weighing the decision, then the door slowly opens.

"I've been worried. Sam too. We miss you."

I don't wait for him to ask me in or to sit. I walk inside, take a seat on the couch and pat the spot next to me. He reluctantly sits.

"I don't want to talk about that day anymore," he says.

"That's understandable. Let's talk about today. What's going on up here?" I tap the side of my head.

"I'm trying to get to a better place. I want to stop with the drinking. It hasn't really solved anything. But it's a struggle. I'm a weak man."

"That's not true. If you can be so brutally broken and still find the courage to be kind to another being, like Sam, then I think you're actually a badass with a heart of gold." My words come easily because it's the truth.

I get a half smile.

"I think you can do whatever you want to. I think you will do it. But maybe we can help by keeping everything between us like it has been. Don't you see? We distract each other from our pain. If only for an hour at a time."

"What if instead my pain adds to yours? Or worse yet, to Sam's."

"You're overthinking it. You're in here too much," I say, pointing to my head. "Being with you feels good to us. It's better having someone else to laugh with and talk to. We relate to each other because we're all damaged. The three of us, Parish, we're like broken playthings on an island of lost toys. And you're the king. We can't abandon our leader."

The look on his face makes me almost cry. He knows I see how deeply he's hurting. And then I do something that wasn't planned. I lean in for a kiss. And I don't stop there.

"I want you. And I want the comfort of sex. We both need it," I say.

He shakes his head and closes his eyes. "No. Not like this. I can't believe I'm saying it, but not now."

"Please, Parish. I've been thinking too much. Help me."

I bring my face close to his, our lips almost touching. I gaze in his beautiful tear-filled eyes. "I want to touch you. I want to feel your hands on my skin. Come on, won't you cut a girl a break?"

He takes my hands in his. "I want you too. You already know that, Scarlett. But I'm not sure I'd be myself today. I can't get out of my mind, and you deserve a man's undivided attention."

How do I politely ask him to slam me against the wall and fuck me senseless? I'm ready for fireworks instead of sparklers. I know this is the man to give them to me. I cut off his stupid words with a nibble on his ear and a tongue trailing down his neck. He stops protesting.

Damn, that smile.

CHAPTER 7

PARISH

*O*ur hands take the lead, reaching for each other before there's time to think things through. I'm on fire and Scarlett's fanning the flames. Didn't plan on it, didn't think I wanted it. Never been so wrong. Wouldn't be surprised if we self-implode with all the pent-up desire straining to get out.

I grab a fistful of her hair and pull it back hard, challenging her with my eyes. You want it? Buckle up, baby. There's the look I was hoping for. Defiance. She's game. The ultimate seduction.

But my lips kissing her neck and nibbling her ear turn gentle. Her natural scent is intoxicating. Deceptively innocent. It tames me for a few seconds, threatening to change the direction of things. Then she gives me some of my own medicine, threading fingers in my hair, and pulling my head back. Hard. It makes me chuckle.

"However you want it," I say.

There's a kind of desperation in the way we go at each other. Our clothes get thrown to the floor as if they're on fire. Our pain has turned to an aggression that needs to be expressed. Released. Scarlett matches me in intensity. There's no wilting flower here and no sign of shyness. It's fucking hot.

Beautiful full breasts, pink aroused nipples, her spectacular ass, and the perfectly formed lips, major and minor. Everything is on display. She's shaved clean. My erect dick and blue balls beg for release.

Our hungry mouths and busy fingers exploring and appreciating it all. Her body's my party. Mine hers.

The fact this side of her was hidden behind sweatshirts and ponytails makes the contradiction all the more striking.

There's an unrehearsed wild dance happening and I'm aroused beyond anything I've experienced before. All five senses are engaged and on alert. What I see ticks every box. What I touch sends a current up and down my spine. It always lands squarely on my dick.

I hear her moans and smell the sweet juices and the aroma of our mingled sweat. But the taste of her sex, oh God. That's the one that should be bottled and sold to men with erectile dysfunction. They'd get it up in no time.

How the hell did I think this might be too sad to be pleasurable? The opposite's true. I can't hold any other thought than the excitement of knowing I'm about to fuck this stunning woman.

"Tell me what you crave. What you really want," she says, offering to fulfill my fantasies.

My dick screams a wordless plea. *Touch me.*

Soft Break

Slowly I come out of a dreamless sleep. Ow. My arm's under Scarlett's head and it feels like it's been there for too long a time. My ass moves for a better position on the couch. We never made it out of the living room. She stirs. I untangle from her.

"We fell asleep," I say, watching her beautiful sleepy face.

Her eyes open slowly and meet mine. She smiles. That's all it takes. I throw back the soft blanket we slept under and look at the treasure beneath. What a body. I kiss soft lips, the cheek, her neck. The response is immediate. Arms encircle my neck and she rolls on top of me.

"Let's go in the bedroom," I say.

"You up for round two?" she asks.

"You're inspiring." I trail my fingers down her back. "How much time do we have?"

"Sam'll be home at three thirty. His friend's mom is giving him a lift."

I look at the clock. "Good. We've got two hours and twenty-three minutes."

As she stands her eyes are on my dick. I give her a wave. She giggles.

"Counting the minutes, are we?"

"I'm going to use every one of them. This time we're gonna take it slow," I say, getting up.

She's all curves, soft in the right places and firm where it counts.

"Let's have some music," she says, walking into the bedroom.

"I don't listen to music. Used to love it, but…"

There's no need to finish the sentence. I'm sure she's done it in her head.

"I've got a playlist on my phone. I'm a Fifty Shades girl. Love the soundtracks. Would that be okay?"

"Haven't a clue what kind of music that is. But if you like it, I'm in."

As she walks out of the room to get the cell, I'm enjoying the perspective. Naked Scarlett walking away from me is my new favorite vista. Fuck the ocean.

I turn back the bedding, get on top and silently thank the god I don't believe in. There's been no other women in this bed, this room, the house. But I'm ready for Scarlett, and nothing about it seems unnatural.

Then I hear the music. As she returns, a slow sexy R&B beat accompanying her, she's dancing. She's good at that too. Sensual. I get no sense of self-consciousness from her as she moves closer.

We may never leave this room.

Setting the phone on the bureau she lifts her hair from her neck and holds it against the back of her head. I watch the way she moves her hips to the rhythm. It's subtle and slow. She gives a naughty crooked grin. Without breaking eye contact, she lifts her breasts and pinches her nipples. A zing goes from my balls to the tip of my dick.

"I like that," I say, touching myself. I'm hard as fuck.

When I take my hand away, it stands proud. Ready.

She climbs onto the end of the bed and crawls toward where I lay. All to the beat of the song, which she's also lip-syncing. I spread my legs.

"Come here, baby," I say.

Scarlett kneels, her mouth hovering above my dick. But instead of touching me, she pretends it's a microphone. I'm her prick prop. Resting on my elbows watching the show, it's funny for a good three seconds. Then my impatience reaches its limit.

I swing my hips and smack her on the cheek. With my dick. We start laughing. But it turns to something new. She gives me this lustful look. The room fades. Her lips part just a little and she flicks her tongue lightly over the head, hands wrapping around my shaft. Oh, yeah. Yeah.

"Get at me," I sigh.

Every man loves a blow job, but this one is above all others. Can a hummer be a religious experience? She takes my generous size in stride, sucking from base to tip and back again. The movement of her hands in coordination with her mouth is unique. Scarlett style.

She's doing this thing that must come naturally to her, but I've never felt the sensation before. It's artistic in some weird sense of the word, a kind of worship woman to man. Just the right amount of pull and pressure.

Her tongue. She's making sure nothing is neglected. My eyes close and I get lost.

Then she moves to my balls and taint. She licks and brings me to the edge of pleasure. I'm not certain I'll be able to hold back if she keeps this up. Things can't go this fast.

"Wait," I say.

My hands reach for her and I bring her forward till we're face to face. In one smooth move I flip her over. Now I'm on top. Our eyes on each other.

"I'm gonna come if you keep doing that thing you do."

"Then come. I want you to."

Oh God. I wouldn't be surprised if she could make me come with her words. No touching, just the sound of her voice and what she says.

"We'll have it all. Today, tomorrow, let's never leave the bed."

A smile lifts the corners of her luscious lips. There's promise behind her eyes, as if a new better world exists for exploration. My eyes linger on hers.

"You're beautiful," I say. "Let me see all of you."

I slowly move down, kissing her breasts as I do, touching the velvety skin, then her stomach and finally the mound. I use my hands to spread her legs. The music reflects the mood. Hot, turned on, and the right tempo for fucking. I'm at the entry to heaven.

She lifts herself to me, impatient for my lips on hers. I use my tongue to tease, and I take in the scent of her. I breathe it and taste the juices. Raising my head to lock eyes with her, I give my review.

"Like honey," I say.

My mouth goes to the source of joy, to show Scarlett I know my way around a woman. Her lips are so beautifully formed, like a new creation from a god who worships the female. When I part them she's all pink and tightly put together, except for the clit which is peeking out from its hood, round and wet with the juices of desire.

Jesus. I love that she's so wet. My fingers run along the lips and

I'm sticky with evidence she wants me. I taste it. I suck her, I run my tongue up and down, in and out, always gently returning to the most-delicate spot.

The sound of Scarlett's moaning is enough to make a man hard. It's not loud and wild. It's contained and makes me think she's holding back because to let it go might shake the house. It's a fucking turn on.

I lift her legs back and hold them there with my hands while I feast on the very essence of her. She helps me by grabbing them and pulling back further, making sure I'm getting the best access.

"Parish. Parish. Like that. Right there," she whisper yells.

I'm worshiping her pussy, knowing she's close. Come on, baby.

Then her body stiffens as the orgasm ascends and breaks loose. My tongue vibrating lightly against her clit. She lets go.

"Ohhhhhhhhhh! Fuck! I'm coming! Oh, oh, oh!"

It goes on and on, bringing her as far as the intense sensation reaches. Her hands go to my head and signal for me to stop. I still my tongue but leave it where it is. She lifts her head and shows me how much she likes that, with a slight lift of her hips which presses her clit against my tongue for one last throb. I feel the pulsating beat.

"What the hell was that, Parish?" she says between breaths.

Lifting myself atop her, I take a few seconds to watch the afterglow on her flushed face. Her breasts rise and fall against my chest. I take one at a time in my mouth. The nipples so fucking erect, the feel of them between my lips and the sound of her erotic sigh keeping my dick hard as steel. I've got to have her.

I steady myself with hands on either side of her shoulders, angling my upper body and slowly grinding against her in a tease. Her pussy meets my movements and she opens her legs in wordless welcome. Arms encircle my torso and fingers glide down the small my back.

We haven't looked away from the pull of each other's eyes. I'm drowning in her stormy sea, happy to be a casualty. I'm just about to put it in.

"Your beautiful cock. Can I ride it?"

No need for words. I flip her over and smile my answer. Fuck me, baby. But she doesn't. She straddles me wide, positioning my dick facing toward me between her legs. The weight of her keeping it flat against my stomach. Then she starts to move. Forward and back, forward and back. Slowly. Up and down the length of my dick. Oh yeah. My God.

The lips are wrapped around the girth of me. Every time she pulls back from the head of my dick they open a little and momentarily reveal the hidden jewel. Christ. There's cum dripping out of her pussy, which makes the slide easy.

Her clit is engorged. I've never been more under a woman's sexual spell. She's moaning. I'm moaning. My fingers play with her breasts and I automatically begin to pump, even though I'm not inside her. I can't take this much longer.

This is the place where holy and unholy merge. An animal in me has risen. As if another of her talents is mind reading, she takes ahold of my dick, lifts herself and positions me at the gate.

Our eyes meet in anticipation of what's about to happen. Where we're going. As gently as possible I sit her down on my dick. She closes her eyes and takes it inch by inch. Feeling the sensation of being inside her makes my heart race. I put my hands on her waist and it takes all my control not to go full force.

We start to fuck.

Ohhhh. It's good like this. Watching a woman who genuinely enjoys sex ride you is unbelievably erotic. She's giving all of herself. Breasts bounce, hips roll, ass moving sensually against me. I could explode into a million pieces of stardust and just be glad I went out this way.

We take it slow at first. The dance of bodies so in sync it feels ordained. Alongside the passion and heat, beside the need and want, stands a new thing. Bigger. There's been a change of some kind. And even my pillow that's been filled with tears, now becomes a soft cradle as I look at Scarlett.

Something never felt before passes from her to me and back again. I have no trouble identifying the impression. It's the feeling this is one of the most purely real moments of my life. One never felt before. This is lovemaking.

CHAPTER 8

SCARLETT

obble, gobble. The phrase skips through my mind and settles on Parish. Wish I was gobbling his mighty drumstick right now. Instead, in a real fish-out-of-water scene, I've got holiday kitchen duty. The arrival of my entire family was the cockblock of the century.

All three of my brothers promised to be here for Sam's first holidays without his parents. They decided not to bring the girlfriends. It's just too intimate of an occasion. None of us know how much crying there will be.

I've been looking forward to their visit for weeks, and I love them beyond words. But the fact it occurred the day after the mind-bending sex fest has put a damper on things. I'm going to make an assumption. Neither of us are anywhere near finished with each other. I've only just begun the tour of his body.

It's not a shocker Parish is choosing to keep his distance.

Meeting the family was never going to happen. I knew that. There's no way I'd press for more than he's ready to give. Sam and I are lucky he's as available as he's been, considering the state he was in when we met. Not to mention our own mindset. When I think of it there was a kind of courage in him taking us on. Sadness on top of sadness.

He couldn't be talked into sharing our Thanksgiving dinner today. Not by me, or even when I brought in the big guns to do the pleading. Sam struck out too.

I'm going to surprise Parish with a dinner delivery later. I've tried to figure a way to bring it myself, and while I'm there offer him a little Scarlett pie dessert. Instead, I'll reluctantly let Sam handle things. Then if anyone sees me making a plate for the neighbor it won't raise any red flags.

My brothers are nosy little shits when it comes to my love life. They love to butt in. All three have tried to dissuade me from wasting time with Harry. Aargon thinks he's annoying, Nobel finds him boring and Van says the guy has one mood, and it's too fucking upbeat. Funny how that review used to piss me off. Now I'm finding it accurate. It's the Parish effect.

I'm giggling under my breath and crying at the same time as I chop onions for today's feast. Everything I think of, everywhere my mind wanders, leads to a dirty thought. There's no reason to pay attention to all the other impressions of that day that try to squeeze their way inside. Like how my heart felt. That's the new sensation I can't put a name to. I'm trying to ignore it.

The memories of three long days ago have replayed a hundred times in my mind. The looks he'd give me, the way his fingers moved through my hair. His eyes when he was coming. I need a fan. Really. Wonder if Kristen has one around here?

What's needed is that I keep things in perspective. Be mindful of our *just friends* status which I demanded firmly. Rightfully. I can't forget the motive was noble. *Think of Sam. Think of Sam.*

But is it so bad allowing myself a little time to stay wrapped in a bubble of bliss? How could something that feels so right be wrong? They're private thoughts. So I'm going to revel in the memories. Everything else is interruption.

I haven't been up this early in years. Probably last time Harry and I traveled. It was to Rio for Carnival. Funny how I feel more excitement here today, looking out the window at the modest house by the sea. Parish is in there.

I imagine he's still sleeping under the white down comforter with the blackout curtains drawn. Or maybe he's in the shower. Oh yeah. That's going to be number one on my list of *Places I Want to Fuck Parish*.

It's been a kind of torture staying away from him. Wonder if he feels the same? Every night when he calls I hear about how hard he gets thinking of me. Last night was surprising. He talked about how he missed our conversations. He said I've been able to soothe the beast that sorrow is. I almost cried. One thrilled heart goes far. His words have carried me all the way to this moment.

At the same time, I'm conscious of making sure to keep my happiness to myself. I can't tell my mom, or my brothers, and definitely not Sam. If I feel the urge to talk it'll be Dad I go to. But it's a moot point because it feels amazing keeping this secret between Parish and me.

The shuffling of my father's footwear on the wooden floor grabs my attention.

"Umm, coffee smells good."

"Morning, Dad."

I love this one-of-a-kind man. He's an interesting guy. Starting with the Uggs he loves to wear. Says they're the most comfortable shoes he's ever worn, and he doesn't give two shits if other people think he looks weird. It used to drive Van crazy when he was a teen. He'd say they were girls' shoes. But Dad won him over eventually.

The rest of him is cool unleashed. It's the artist living inside him. That and the fact he's French. Never lost his accent or its effect on women. Especially the only one he loves most. My mother. From the ice-blue eyes to the long waves of salt and pepper hair to the bracelets stacked on his wrist, he's cool. With hands made rough from years of working with clay and a

THE BEACH IN WINTER

hundred other mediums for his sculptures. His artistic nature is always on display.

This morning look brings back memories. Baggy running pants, open short robe, his stomach sticking out. I chuckle under my breath at the only visual that contradicts his cool. The big belly. There's always a handkerchief sticking from his pants pocket. It's practically a uniform. When I was a teenager it used to embarrass me. What fools the young can be when our vision of things is so limited.

"I heard you laughing. Didn't think you were in here alone," he says, pouring himself a mug. "What's so funny?"

I scoop the onions into a baggie and seal it shut, avoiding eye contact when I lie.

"Nothing. I was just remembering something Sam said," I say, tossing the bag into the refrigerator.

His eyes are on me, sizing up my response. I know it without looking. Gaston Lyon is a master at busting his children's fibs. Doesn't matter we're all adults. When he doesn't question the veracity of my statement I relax.

Coming to my side, he takes me in an embrace and kisses the top of my head.

"You know how proud of you we are? Your mother and I, your brothers, we're all incredibly proud."

Oh shit. A lump rises in my throat. I'm afraid if I speak it will turn into tears, so I just nod against his chest.

"Don't think we can't see what a sacrifice this is in your life. But just as you've always done, you jumped in with both feet. And most impressive of all Scarlett, is that you do it with such a loving attitude. I'm impressed beyond words, little girl."

His familiar name for me hits the mark.

"Thanks, Dad," I choke out the words.

"Kristen is watching over you, I'm sure. And she's happy you're taking such good care of her boy."

73

That does it. We both start crying. My face is buried in his chest, he's patting my back.

"What the hell's this? You two can't be trusted alone. Always crying."

Aargon enters the kitchen fully dressed and groomed. I expect nothing less from my oldest brother. He looks like he stepped out of a men's fashion magazine. As if he has a stylist and a hair person at his disposal. The fact he's so good looking doesn't hurt the image.

"Shut up. Your sister and I are having a moment," my father says.

Wiping my nose with the hankie he just offered, and trying to get my shit together, I change the subject. "Where's Mom? She's usually up by now."

"Right here."

We hear her calling from the living room, coming closer to the kitchen.

"Gobble, gobble my family."

Like robots, the three of us return her Thanksgiving greeting as she walks in the room. It hits me that she and Aargon are two of a kind stylistically. Always put together, classic, and so different from the rest of us. They're both camera ready while I'm still in my sweats.

"Gaston, I see you're wearing your formal wear for the occasion," she says, tucking a silver curl behind an ear.

The words are delivered as if she's making a joke, but everyone here knows the message. It's the same one that's been passed between them for forty-three years. She crosses to Aargon and kisses him on the cheek.

"Um, Mom? I think that ship has sailed. Dad's pretty clear about liking the casual look," Aragon says chuckling.

"Besides, we're at the beach! Shorts and the whole relaxed thing works," I say.

My father grins and shoots his wife a self-satisfied look.

THE BEACH IN WINTER

"Thank you, children. Your old dad appreciates your support."
My mother takes it like she always has. It's what they do. She protests about something he does, he doesn't listen. I believe it's their dance. She's charmed by her man. And he by her. It's kinda awesome to watch. I think her logical, scientific way of looking at things was thrown out the window when they met in France all those years ago. I pretty much believe she found him irresistible.

"By the way Aurora, you look very sexy this morning."

"Thank you, darling," she says, moving to his side.

They embrace and kiss good morning in a familiar move. It always looks as if it's going to lead further. But thankfully to their children, it doesn't.

With that, Aargon looks at me and pinches his lips together in protest. I start laughing.

"I feel like we're back on Franklin Street getting ready for school," I say.

"Morning, everyone. Coffee, give me coffee."

Nobel walks in still half asleep, green eyes at half-mast. His thick head of chocolate hair is sticking up as usual. He's still wearing pajama bottoms with a wrinkled hoodie.

"Morning darling boy," my mother says, taking his face in her hands and kissing his cheek.

"Teddy still sleeping?" my father says, pulling up a barstool at the island.

Aargon takes the seat next to him. "Yeah. Your grandson would sleep till noon every day if I'd let him."

Taking the huge turkey out of the refrigerator I get it to the counter and weigh in. "He and Sam haven't seen each other in such a long time. You two weren't here for Thanksgiving last year, right?"

In a flash I see the expressions shift. We're thinking of past holidays and the fact it was Kristen's favorite. The one she hosted every year.

My mother's eyes fill with tears. When my dad notices he gets

75

up and takes her against him. It's a wordless comfort and all that can be done. We've said and offered every show of sympathy and empathy. We've soothed each other's souls as much as humanly possible. Still, we're raw.

This is the first of the many holidays and celebrations we'll have to go through without the one we love.

Thankfully Van shows up to stop our train of thought. He reads the room and heads for the coffee without a word.

"Van, pull up your pants! Otherwise your pee pee's going to escape," my mother says.

Okay we needed that. It makes all of us laugh except for Van, who looks down at his loose pajama bottoms.

"Is it still necessary to use pee pee?" Nobel says, lifting an eyebrow. "We're almost forty years old."

"Quit looking, Mom! What the hell?" Van says. "And speak for yourself, Nobel. I'm thirty-six."

Here we go.

"It's pretty hard to miss when your child is going to lose his pants. There's ladies here, you know," Mom says.

"It's just Scarlett. Crap."

"And your mother. I saw enough of it when you were a kid," she says.

The fact Van used to run naked through the house at the drop of a hat when he was little doesn't escape any of us. Nothing he does surprises us, even now.

"Pull them up," my father says.

Van finds the whole exchange funny. But he tugs up his pants and tightens the cord.

"Okay, if we're finished talking about Van's dick, let's get this started. I've got her recipes right here, and I need all the help I can get," I say, trying with all my might to permanently change our mood.

"Aargon, you get the two boxes in the garage marked Thanksgiving. Let's put up the decorations for Sam," my mother says.

I've been overruled about the decorations. After the first misstep of removing the familiar things in the house.

More than one of us sighs at the thought of a Thanksgiving without our Kristen.

This is going to be tough.

Scene Break

Uncomfortable. That's the word I'd use to describe what's happening here. And false. Every person here's trying to fake a happy holiday. Well, all except Sam. He's letting it show on his face, which makes us all feel helpless.

A minute ago I saw Teddy offer his cousin the prized last turkey wing. Sam just shook his head no. They fought over them in years past. It's almost tradition. It made me want to cry to see the helpless look on Teddy's face.

My father's handiwork is evident on the beautifully laid table. Kristen's ceramic turkey collection stretches down the center, just like always. The tablecloth and napkins her favorites. Traditional holiday plates were used. The glass bowl filled with Sam's sea glass collection is in the center. My sister loved that touch.

Thanks to my mother and father, the recipes were followed to the letter. I can't imagine what would have become of the meal if I had to wing it. But everything tasted different. And even the conversations have been stilted. Missing is the free flow of words and laughs, the teasing. The Lyon meals were where the best memories were made. Is it gone now? Will we ever be unaware of our great loss?

"So Sam, how's your friend Father Campbell?" my dad says, attempting to divert the conversation. "Is he still taking the kids fishing?"

"I don't know," Sam replies.

What? Who's he talking about? I've never heard Sam talking about him.

"Haven't you seen him at church?" Mom says.

Oh shit. Church. I completely forgot they'd all go to church on Sundays.

"Sam, you never said anything. I'm sorry I forgot," I say.

Everyone looks at me. But with empathy. No one's judging. Except maybe Sam.

"Would you like to start going again? I could take you, no problem."

He just shakes his head. Shit, fuck. Tears well in his eyes. Then in all our eyes.

The doorbell saves us. Three people rise from their chairs at once, trying to be the lucky one who gets to leave the table.

"I got it," Van says, beating his father and brother.

In my heart of hearts I'm hoping it's Parish. He's practically the only one it could be. Maybe he's had a change of heart. He'll be the perfect distraction.

When the door squeaks open a familiar voice calls out.

"Surprise!"

Harry's call sounds through to the dining room and by the looks on my family's faces they think I'm pleased, even though they're not. Crap.

"Look who the turkey dragged in," Van says, leading the way back into the room. A beaming Harry throws his arms open at the sight of the holiday spread. He's got his favorite wool coat on with the scarf he told me makes his blue eyes look really good.

"Hi, everyone! The party's here!"

Clearly this man is awful at reading the room.

Annoying. That's the only word I can think of right now. What the fuck? There's no choice but to get up and greet the interloper.

"What are you doing here? I didn't expect you." I say it like I'm pleasantly shocked. In reality I'm not in the mood for his perkiness. It's wildly inappropriate today.

He leans in for a kiss. I turn my head and it lands awkwardly half on my lips and half at the edge of my chin.

I know he must be questioning my move, but I'll be damned if

I'm going to look in his eyes. And I'm not going to kiss lips that don't belong to my neighbor. Surprising even me, that's my new code of conduct.

"Thought I'd surprise you," he says, narrowing his eyes. "The ski trip fell through. You sounded lonely when we talked a few weeks ago. I knew you were disappointed."

I want to tell him I solved that problem. Surprise.

"Grab that chair and pull it up here," my dad says, motioning to the space he's creating between us.

"Help yourself to the feast, Harry," my mother says.

I know she's picked up my mood and if I had to bet I'd say my brothers have too. But none of them have figured out why.

"No, no. I was hungry and picked up something at the airport. I ate in the Uber. Got to keep my figure."

He chuckles at his lame joke and pats his tight abs.

Van pushes his chair back and tosses his napkin to the table. "How long are you here for?"

"Just a few days. I've got to be back on Saturday."

Harry hasn't acknowledged Sam. Hasn't asked how he's doing. It's like he isn't sitting at the table. I don't like that.

"I'm going for a walk on the beach," Sam says.

"No pie?" Dad asks.

"No. I'm done."

"Wait. I'll go with you," Aargon says scraping his chair back.

Mom stands. "Hold on, I'll get my coat."

"I'm in," I say looking to Harry.

He nods. "Yeah sure, let's do it."

There's strength in numbers. My hope is if Parish is looking out his window he won't be able to tell Harry isn't part of the family. I'm going to leave my hands in my pocket and do a lot of talking. There'll be no PDA with my visitor.

Not going to happen.

CHAPTER 9

PARISH

*C*old wind sweeps over my face and cools my temperature as I jog along the shore. The ocean is especially beautiful today. Wild and loud. My nose is running, and everything hurts. It feels great. I chuckle at the illogical, contradictory thought.

I'm conscious of the stiffness in my knees and back. There's no ignoring the aches. My legs are weaker than before. No mystery. A man can't spend five years sitting on his ass and not have it affect ability and strength. Being forty-three plays into the mix as well. How much I'm not sure. Is this what old feels like? Have I already arrived?

Memories of another day argues the point. Earlier in the week I was proving youth. I fucked like a twenty-year-old with an additional twenty-three years' experience. Turned out to be a killer combo. Although it would be wrong to take credit. It was all Scarlett's doing.

Wonder if she's like that with other men? I don't want to believe it. What we did seemed organic and a result of the moment. I think it came from what we are together. Not from habit or personal styles. Scarlett and I created what happened in that bed. End of story.

Bed. God, the woman can move. That thing she did on top. I twitch with the memory of her pussy lips gliding along my dick. I'll be requesting a repeat of that scene. Next time. I hope it's a given, because to think having her in my bed was a one-time event is unacceptable.

What took place triggered a change in me. I'm not acting like myself, but I'm more me than I've ever been. I'm lighter in a way I don't recognize. Not completely rid of the cold thoughts, but better. Maybe I forgot how peaceful it is to not be in a dark emotional state every fucking minute of the day.

Up to now I haven't been able to find my way out. Even self-medicating with whiskey didn't erase the feeling of being stabbed repeatedly in the heart. Alcohol was only a dulling of the knife's blade.

Is it coincidence after being with Scarlett my drinking has slowed? Even more than it had since we met. For the last few days I'm down to three beers at night. And I've started running again. I don't want to put too fine a point on it, because it's only a few days behavior. *Don't get ahead of yourself.*

There is one undeniable truth. What happened when we were together. The feeling I had of being swept away. It's more powerful than my urges to hide or cry or bury myself in the grief. Nothing has done that before.

Careful. I'm always just one bad day or drunken stupor away from old habits. I can't ignore the truth and confuse feeling better for being permanently changed. Everything I've observed about other drinkers has proved that. The fact I want to think I'm different is actually just one more red flag.

I forcefully push a sigh out. It's all that self-reflection crowding my mind. *Enough.*

Up ahead, coming over the dune, I spot a crowd of people walking my way. What's this? I've never seen this many people on our beach. Is that Scarlett? Oh God, it's gotta be her entire family. They've spotted me because I see Sam running my way.

Shit. I'm not good at small talk with strangers. Well, with the recent exception of my new neighbors.

There's another kid running behind Sam, but he catches up to him quickly.

I slow the pace and bring my heart rate to a lower level as the boys get close.

"Hi," Sam calls when he's within shouting distance.

I lift a hand in their direction acknowledging the approach.

The two red-faced boys join me in my cool down.

"Hey," I manage to get out between breaths.

"You're running again. I saw you out here yesterday," Sam says.

I nod my agreement.

"Who's this?" I say, eyes on the taller, thinner, but I think younger boy.

Sam turns to look at the face of the kid. "My cousin, Teddy."

"Hi, Ted," I say.

The kid's face lights up when he hears the shortened version of his name. Maybe he's over the Teddy moniker.

"Did you have Thanksgiving dinner already?" Sam asks.

"Nah. I'm going to make a sandwich after I shower. Did you?"

Ted picks a rock up and tries to skim it across a wave. It's swallowed by crest of foam.

"Yeah. We just finished. Well, almost. Aunt Scarlett's boyfriend showed up and interrupted dessert. But I didn't want anything anyway."

What's this?

My heart starts beating as if I've resumed running.

"Boyfriend? I thought she said she didn't have one."

Sam's watching my face, gaging my reaction. But I'm finding it hard to play cool.

"You said you didn't like him much. Did she change her mind and invite him for the holiday?"

I say it like it's an off-the-cuff comment. But Sam sees right through me.

Shit.

I don't get an answer because the group is approaching and Sam quiets. Good looking family. The bear of a man with long hair is probably the father. I could pick out her brothers easily. They all look like the mother, whose body language is telling me she's still into her husband. And he into her. Their arms are linked and her palm's on his chest.

The one figure sticking out like a sore thumb is the guy on Scarlett's left. Mr. Preppy with the scarf tied too purposely. I bet he took his time making it lay just so. Dick. Just doesn't blend in. He's tall and okay looking and in fairly good shape, but there's something about him I don't like.

"Parish! Hi. Happy Thanksgiving," says Scarlett.

"Hi. Yeah, it's turkey day."

Okay, that sounded idiotic.

"I want to introduce my family. This is my mother, Aurora, and my dad, Gaston," she says, pointing to the parents.

"Hello, nice to meet you both," I say, shaking her father's hand. It's rough and strong, but his smile's warm like his daughter's.

"Sam tells us you're the cool writer who lives in the house next door," Aurora says.

"I don't know about cool, but yeah I'm a writer."

I'm pretty sure I saw Mr. Preppy roll his eyes. Fuck you, asshole.

Scarlett takes the arm of the tallest guy.

"These are my brothers. This is Aargon. Next to him is Van and that's Nobel."

We all do the minimum required. We're friendly but I don't think any of us are the types to glad hand or have an extended conversation with someone we've just met. My kind of guys.

"And this is Harry."

Harry extends his hand and when I go to shake it he squeezes a little too long and hard. Really guy? Are you that unsure of yourself? I return the greeting, grasping his palm and holding

83

tight till I see his shoulder dip. He lets go just in time. My grip's
throbbing.

"Good to meet you, Harry." I say it with a grin. *You little cock-
roach.* The thought this guy was with Scarlett just pisses me off in
general. I know I have no reason to play the jilted lover, but it's
hard not looking out for her. He's not good enough. That's just my
sense of things.

"You too, man." He puffs out the words along with his chest.

On the spot I decide to hear the truth. I don't want to think
about this all night.

"So, are you a cousin?" I say.

Harry smirks and delivers his blow. "No, I'm not. I guess I'm
the boyfriend."

He puts an arm around Scarlett's shoulders. She looks uncomfortable.

"If you have to guess I'd say you might be mistaken," I say with
a chuckle.

Van lets loose one loud laugh, Sam and Teddy are frozen in
their places and Harry's face is turning a nice shade of red. Scarlett's mouth is half open. Looks like she's holding her breath. In
fact everyone does, with the exception of horrible Harry.

"Okay, it was nice meeting Scarlett's family and friend," I say
without looking at the pissed off guy to my right. "I'm going to
head back. Hey Sam, I got that book for you if you want to pick it
up later. Or tomorrow. Either one."

"It was good meeting you, Parish. I'm sure we'll see you again,"
Aurora says.

"You too. Bye, guys."

Seven goodbyes come my way. One is conspicuously absent. I
turn and jog away slowly, knowing at least two sets of eyes are
on me.

Scene Break

A shower did nothing to erase the memory of another man

84

touching Scarlett. As a result, I could spend the entire day standing at the slider looking at the ocean. The urge to have a drink rears its ugly head. That shows me how tenuous my newfound semi-sobriety is.

Think, Parish. Use some of that self-reflection to figure out what's happening between you two. I know it without dissecting every moment of the scene on the beach. The guy had his arm around her. She didn't move or take it off her shoulders. Okay. It's possible I've read too much into the situation. Or maybe I'm so desperate to move into a new phase of life I've created a false narrative.

There's no firm ground for me to stand on here. We're not a couple, she had a life before meeting me. Just because I've been a loner doesn't mean she has. Maybe I'm making too much of it all. The guy, her non response and most of all our time together.

Being clear about it or not, it's making me turn toward my old standby. Alcohol. I need a distraction. Time to write. Walking to my desk I'm suddenly conscious of the fact I haven't looked in the drawer yet today, and not at all yesterday. Hmm. No. I don't feel like it today either. Instead I imagine Justin on that day, but when we built the sandcastle.

The muffled sound of my cell carries all the way from the laundry closet. Shit. They're in the pocket of my running pants. I move quickly to the hallway and retrieve the phone.

"Hello?"

"Parish. It's Gayle."

God. My sister.

"It's John too," my brother says.

I'm too shocked to speak for a few beats. There's a tightening in my throat and my eyes instantly fill with tears. I walk to the kitchen and take the bottle of whiskey from the cupboard. One drink.

"Hello, you two," I say quietly.

"Don't blame John. He wasn't sure we should do this. But when I found the right number I wanted him to hold my hand while I called."

"How are you, brother?" John says softly.

I want to collapse into myself until I figure out how I feel. I know one thing though. It's good hearing their voices again. Overwhelming.

"You still there?" Gayle asks.

"Yeah. Just trying to process what's happening."

I pour myself two fingers of liquid courage and take the first sip. Oh yeah. That's good.

"We miss you, Parish. So much," John says softly.

"I'm gonna be a grandmother. Perry and his wife are expecting."

Gayle surprises me with that one.

"What? We can't be that old," I say with a touch of lightness.

"Well, John's old as shit. He turned fifty this year. Me, I'm still in my fabulous forties," she says with fake attitude. "We lit a birthday candle for your forty-third on March seventeenth. We've done that every year."

My heart aches a little with her words. My stomach is tight and I feel a headache coming on. This is beginning to be too much. But I don't want to hurt them anymore. I love them.

"I hope you let us call you once in a while, brother."

"Please, Parish. I promise not to overdo it. We just don't want to be without you. Please let us back in," Gayle says.

"We'll take whatever you're willing to give. Once a month, once a week. You set the rules."

John was always the negotiator of the three of us. I'm on the verge of actually crying as I take a bigger swig.

"Okay. I've got your numbers. I'll call when..." The catch in my throat gives my shaky emotional state away.

"Call whenever you feel like saying hello. It can be a two

THE BEACH IN WINTER

minute conversation. We're going to do whatever you want," Gayle says, sniffling.

"Yeah. I will. Listen, it was great hearing your voices. I hope you understand it was never about you. I've been so..."

"It doesn't matter. We love you, brother," John says, cutting off my excuses.

His voice cracks with the emotion we're all feeling. We've missed each other. My feelings were tapped down, trapped under crushing grief. Today for the first time in years I'm trying to dig myself free.

Soft Break

My eyes open slowly to the low light in the room. It's changed dramatically. Shit, it's almost six o'clock. I've been out for two hours. No surprise. I drank myself to sleep. Not to unconsciousness, I didn't have the will for that, but into the escape sleep brings.

Ow, my back has a kink. I wasn't sitting right. And shit, the whiskey spilled on the couch. It won't be easy getting that out. It stretches from one cushion to the edges of the next.

My slide backwards wasn't worth the few hours of relief it brought. I should have toughed it out, because now I feel worse than I did before.

Getting up I try to stretch myself straight. Jesus, I feel shitty. My stomach, heartburn, head. It's as if the effect of drinking too much has multiplied.

The phone call threw me and not just because we haven't spoken in so long. The bigger blow is I'm beginning to see the mistake I've made. Neither brother nor sister deserved what I did to them. Their pain today was obvious. But I didn't detect any sign of blame. They don't hold it against me. Unbelievable.

The cell sounds breaking my reverie. Scarlett.

"Hello."

"Your voice. What's wrong?"

"Nothing. Just woke up." I clear my throat hoping to hide my alcohol-affected vocal cords and sit my ass back down.

"So, did you have any turkey?" she says.

"Did you get rid of yours?"

There's a pause before she answers. "What?"

"Your boyfriend. Is he staying with you?"

"I wanted to clear that up. You left before I had the chance. Actually, I wouldn't have done it there anyway, but the truth is he's not my boyfriend."

Okay. So far so good.

"None of my business," I say not meaning it.

"Whether it's your business or not doesn't change the fact. He's not my boyfriend."

"Does he know that?"

"He does now," she says giggling.

That puts a smile on my face and something resembling hope in my heart. Hope for what I don't know. It just feels good.

"Is he still there?"

"No. He decided to fly back tonight. He left about ten minutes ago."

"Well what're you waiting for? Get your ass over here."

"I can't. My whole family's here for a few days and we're gonna play some games in a few minutes."

"You and I should be playing our games."

"You're very naughty."

"You can spank me if you'd like," I say chuckling. "I'll pull my pants down as soon as you walk in the door. Come on, can't you sneak out for twenty minutes?"

She starts giggling and I love the sound. "Twenty minutes? Slam, bam, thank you ma'am, much? Is that all the foreplay I'd get?"

"Listen, I'll spend as long as your body can take. I'll go down on you for five hours if that's what you love."

THE BEACH IN WINTER

The giggle again. "Are those my choices? Twenty minutes or five hours?"

"Scarlett, I liked having you in my bed. I want you to be there again. For as short or long as you want."

There's silence for a few seconds. Then she sighs. "Unfortunately, I'm here for the night. But if you look out your window you should see Sam. He's on his way with a plate and goodie bag for you."

Before I have time to respond, I hear his steps. I turn to see Sam with the goods, ringing the doorbell. Shit. I look like a drunk.

Getting up, I run my hands through my hair. That's all I have time for before opening the door.

"Hey, Sam. What've you got there?"

He walks inside not waiting for an invitation. I'm handed the goods.

"Aunt Scarlett made this for you. There's cookies in the bag."

The way he's looking at my face says a thousand words. I must look like shit.

"Thanks. Come in. Tell me about your day. Having fun with your family?"

As we sit on the couch I spot the half-empty whiskey bottle on the edge of the coffee table. Crap. He spots it too.

"I guess so."

"I'm not feeling great. I've got this headache," I say, rubbing my temples for affect.

"You have that book you told me about?"

Thank God for diversion. "Oh yeah, let me get it."

I walk to my desk and take the book in hand. "This is my first in the Daniel Dustin series. Your aunt gave me the go ahead for you to read it, as long as we discuss it when you do."

"Yeah, she told me."

"You could make notes if you have questions. Or we can talk about each chapter. Whatever you want."

But he's not paying attention. His eyes are on the whiskey bottle.

"You don't drive when you have that, right?"

Fuck me. The kid's thinking of his parents' accident. The drunk driver who ended it all.

"Never, Sam. Promise."

I don't get a smile or nod or any hint of what he's thinking. Except for the reflection of pain in his eyes.

"It's a crutch I've made the mistake of using to help me through. It fails miserably. I'm trying not to do that as much anymore, but today I slipped back."

It's unnerving when a child looks into your soul and sees you for what you are.

"Can I sit on your porch and read?" he says softly.

"Really? What about your family? They're here for the holiday, right?"

He dips his chin and his mouth twists. "I don't want to celebrate any of the holidays this year."

"I understand that. I bet they'd all give you a pass to feel whatever way you want. Have you told them?"

I get a shake of the head.

"They're just trying to be there for you, Sam. Take it from me. When you're ready they'll be waiting. In the meantime, do whatever you want. Just remember they're suffering too."

He takes a seat on the couch and I follow his lead.

"Grandma and Aunt Scarlett ask me too many questions. They always want to know how I'm doing."

"It's coming from a kind place. Women are usually more expressive than us guys. But I hear ya. What about your uncles? Are you close?"

"Uncle Aargon is kind of serious. But he's nice. Nobel is good, he sends me music he likes. Van is the funniest. He's my favorite I guess. He's kinda wild. They all live in Montana so we don't see each other very much."

"What you need is to have a guys' night. Play cards maybe. No girls allowed. Ask your grandpa too."

He rolls the idea around.

"Can you come?" he says with hope in his voice.

I didn't think this through. I see no way out.

"Yeah, of course."

Damn. The kid looks happy.

CHAPTER 10

SCARLETT

*R*aucous male laughter carries from the dining room all the way into my bedroom. The night after Thanksgiving is turning into a party. For those in the other room, that is. Mom and I are stretched out on my bed looking through the box of precious photographs Kristen had tucked away in her closet.

Every so often we eavesdrop on the men. It's always interesting hearing how they talk to each other when they're alone in testosteroneville. According to Sam, there's a strict *No Girls Allowed* policy tonight.

It's true, men are better than women at accessing their younger selves. They revert as soon as they're in a group. There's teasing and smack talk, and a few minutes ago we heard a burping contest. Somehow it makes them happy. I'm not sure they ever completely leave being twelve behind. Tonight Sam gets initiated into the club.

"Somebody said something funny. Your father's having hysterics."

"No doubt Van's offering something inappropriate."

"I hope they use common sense and don't say anything too mature in front of Sam," my mother says.

My head turns to her and our eyes meet. I'm looking at her like she's crazy. We burst out laughing at her statement.

"You're nuts if you think Van's going to hold back anything."

She hangs her head in mock despair. "I know."

Even Parish and Aargon's laughs can be heard over our conversation. That's encouraging. I didn't expect it from Parish, and rarely have I heard it from Aargon. Not since he lost his wife. He was always serious, but her death a decade ago sealed joy inside him. Tonight's fun may be helping more than one sad heart. If just for a few hours. It makes me believe in possibilities.

The only voice I haven't heard is Sam's. I'm sure he's having a good time though.

"We're banished from the party, but it's very entertaining," I say, tilting my head to hear better.

"I don't mind. Sometimes the boys need alone time. I'll be back," she says, getting up and heading for the bathroom.

To think my brothers and father are having a good time with Parish pleases me a little too much. If I'm so sure he's not boyfriend material I shouldn't give a damn. But I do. I mean I'm not officially dating him. Pretty sure screwing the man doesn't count as dating.

I did let my family know he's been a good neighbor and more importantly kind to Sam. I conveniently left out the drinking and occasionally passing out on the sand part of the story. Even just thinking of it now makes me nervous. Because, even though I haven't seen any sign of that behavior lately, it's still a recent reality. And the more I want him the bigger the waving red flag.

When Sam told me about plans for poker night I almost choked on my turkey sandwich. Finding out it was Parish's idea was an even greater shock. Then last night he explained what went behind the discussion.

It was another example of how he puts Sam before himself, even though their friendship's new. I know it's because he's been a father. Could be the sense of tenderness and compassion never leaves a man.

My mother returns and reclaims her spot next to me on the bed.

"Okay, let's keep going."

Here in my room, Mom and I are opening the wound we share and facing how it's hobbled us. Another difference between men and women. We consider crying to be our friend. Tonight in between tears there's laughter. It's an emotional roller coaster as we navigate memories.

One picture grabs us and rips our hearts, the next brings back better days spent together, when we swam, or skied or just sat around the family table enjoying being alive together.

"Oh, look at her. She looked beautiful that night," my mother says, looking at Kristen's prom picture, senior year.

"That was the night she lost her virginity," I say.

"I know. She told me."

"I'm impressed. Very brave of her," I say, lifting an eyebrow.

"She was thirty when she told me," my mother says chuckling. "Bravery had nothing to do with it."

"That makes so much more sense," I giggle.

She looks at me with an expression I recognize from my teen years. Here comes a pointed question.

"So tell me about this man."

"What man?"

"The handsome mysterious one you're trying to sell as your friend."

She's so damn smart. I can't hold my straight face. A smile lifts the corners of my mouth.

"I knew I was right," she says. "Your whole demeanor changes when you talk about him."

"We're having a flirt. Nothing more."

She just sits with my statement for a while. Her logical scientific mind dissecting the information I've presented.

THE BEACH IN WINTER

"Now tell me the true story," she says, ignoring my denial.

I hesitate for a moment before spilling my guts.

"Okay. We're attracted to each other, and we've acted on it, once. Sam doesn't know and never will."

"For what reason? I mean that's a good instinct, but what's behind it?"

I get off the bed and start pacing, my nervous tell.

"For a few reasons. Parish is still grieving the death of his child."

"Oh, that's a tough one. Maybe you can heal together."

"Mostly my hesitation is because I can't have Sam become attached to a man who suddenly may not be in his life."

Her head's nodding before the words leave her mouth. She takes my hand.

"He's suffered enough separation for a lifetime. And putting him ahead of yourself is what needs to happen. But don't forget you need a life too. You'll sense when it's time."

"But meanwhile I don't see the harm in having a good pop pop," I say, knowing my mother will decipher the code.

She twists her mouth in response. "It feels like more."

"You're reading too much into it, Mom."

"Want to know what I see?"

"What?"

"This one is all man. You usually gravitate toward men that are still half boy. Maybe you're selling him short, Scarlett."

My mother the former chemical engineer has gathered the evidence, observed the reaction of the tested objects each to the other and come to her hypothesis. Damn science.

Scene Break

Walking down the school hallway toward Mrs. Clark's office is a flashback to my Fremont Grammar School days. The sound of chattering children, the smell of chalk. I think this is my third visit. Yeah. First time introductions, last time was to set up my schedule.

Who knew parents had to volunteer their time in some capacity? I'm not working so there was no quick excuse when told. Besides I want Sam to know I'm all in. In every way, including the ones I'd rather take a pass on. It's a huge job trying to do everything by the book. An impossible one. Every day I remind myself to just aim for an inch better than I did the day before.

Hey, there's that redheaded kid I used to see with Sam when I'd visit. Pete. He was always at the house. Wonder why he hasn't been around?

"Hi!" I say as he passes me without a glance. "It's Pete, right?"

He turns. Eyebrows knit together. There's absolutely no recognition in his pretty blue eyes.

"I'm Scarlett. Sam's aunt. We met at the big Fourth of July beach party. You stayed at the house. I think it was two or three years ago. Remember?"

"Uh, yeah I think so."

"I'm sure Sam would love to have you come to the house. You could stay the night if your parents okay it."

I'm not sure what I expected in response, but it wasn't this. He gets this pained look on his face. Before I have a chance to respond, he turns and walks away. My jaw drops as I watch him blend into the crowd and disappear around the corner.

"Scarlett!"

I turn to see Mrs. Clark.

"Hi. I was just headed to your office," I say.

"I thought I'd head you off. We're going to go to Mr. Paladino's office. He'd like to speak with you."

"The principal?"

"I asked for his input. This way," she says, guiding me to the last door on the right. His name is on the plaque hanging over the doorway.

"Here we go. He's expecting us."

She knocks and opens the door without waiting for an answer, allowing me to enter first.

I kind of feel like I did back in nineteen ninety-six when I got sent to the principal's office for laughing at Scott O'Neil's jokes in class. It was the fact I couldn't stop that sealed my fate.

A younger than I imagined nice-looking man sits behind a modest desk. On the walls are pictures of Teachers of the Year.

"Miss Grace. So happy to meet you," he says, rising and extending his hand.

We shake. I think I recognize the look he's giving me. It's subtle but unmistakable. He likes what he sees. Sorry guy. I am otherwise engaged. But it won't hurt to have Sam's principal in our corner.

"Nice to meet you as well, Principal Paladino. What's this about?"

"Sit. Please."

I take a seat and he and Mrs. Clark follow.

"First of all, let me say I'm aware of your situation. It must be an overwhelming time for both you and Sam."

"Thank you. Yes, I'm new at it all. But we seem to be settling into our new normal."

"We understand it's a process, but we just want to make sure you're aware of some of Sam's behaviors."

Uh oh.

"And we also want to make sure we're all on the same page, working together to make this transition as smooth as possible," Mrs. Clark says.

An uneasy feeling begins to rise.

"What's this about?"

Mr. Paladino has a compassionate look on his face as he lays it all out.

"The last day of school, before Thanksgiving break, Sam was walking with some boys in the corridor and bumped into a teacher. It was Mrs. Rogers, who teaches seventh grade."

"Yes," I say, waiting for the other shoe to drop.

"He started laughing and didn't offer an apology. So she stopped him and let him know it was unacceptable."

"Well good. She did the right thing. I will definitely speak with him."

Mrs. Clark pats my hand. "That's not all."

"Sam's response was to tell her to fuck off."

I feel my face turning red. And I'm remembering saying fuck with him in my sister's room. At my request.

"Oh my God. I'm so sorry. Are you sure that's what was said?"

The principal stares at me like he must have a hundred other parents who doubt their sweet children could be guilty.

"Yes. Many people heard it."

"I'm shocked. Sam barely talks at home. He's mostly to himself. I work at engaging him every day. Really I do."

"I've no doubt you're doing a good job, Miss Lyon. It's such unusual traumatic circumstances. We need to work together here."

"Yeah, of course. What was his punishment? He never stayed after school that I was aware of anyway. I pick him up every day."

"We went another route. We had him meet with Mrs. Rogers and myself. We told him his behavior was unacceptable and would only be excused one time. We made sure he knew it was because we were mindful of his loss and its effect. He apologized and there were tears."

My shoulders slump with the image of the scene. Suddenly I'm tired, and it's only two o'clock.

"We want to keep you abreast of what we've noticed as far as Sam's concerned," Mrs. Clark says.

"I need to know. Is there more?"

"Yes."

"Since his return to school, his grades and compositions have reflected the harsh reality of his situation. He used to like writing stories and was a better-than-average student. But now there's been changes. He does the bare minimum and sometimes less than that. Nothing we've done has made an impact. Do you work with him on his homework?"

Shit.

"Uh, he's never asked me for help. I ask if he's done his homework and he always says yes."

I hear how stupid that sounds as soon as the words leave my mouth.

"And he's gravitating toward new friends. Boys that he never befriended before. He's ignoring the ones he had and trying to blend in with kids that are, well let's just say, troubled. Even in eighth grade Scarlett there are children on the wrong path or headed in the wrong direction. Those are the ones he's seeking out," Mr. Paladino says.

Now I see why Pete looked sad. Sam's abandoned the friendship.

"He's always been such a great kid," Mrs. Clark says.

"He's never asked for my help. I just assumed he was handling everything. Oh God, I should have watched closer."

They both make appropriate responses that I'm not to blame, and that the important thing is we proceed together as a unit. But I've dropped the ball. I see it now.

Scene Break

All the way home and into the house, I'm trying to form a plan. I didn't expect this sort of thing to come up so soon. If at all. Shouting expletives in grammar school seems so aggressive. But what do I know? I've been too busy taking charge of a thousand new jobs that don't really matter. The cooking, the house, making sure he's wearing clean clothes. There wasn't time to look deeper.

It's taken every day being in this strange world to be aware of just the things on the surface. There's so much information to take in. I don't want to react too quickly and get it wrong. I've got to get this first disciplinary stance right.

But if Sam's really spiraling and hanging with shady kids that influence him there isn't time to wait. And am I too quick to blame the other boys? It's his own decisions that shape his life. My mother said that to me many times when I'd get cornered and try to blame my behavior on someone else.

Her and my father's words have played in my head over and over the last few months. You never know how deep-seated they are till you have a child to care for. My God. I've got a child.

I need to get in the shower and wash away the dread. A brilliant idea occurs to me as I'm unbuttoning my pants and walking into the bedroom. Parish. I need his input. And not just verbally. In the back of my mind I hear Luther Vandross crooning "Sexual Healing." I hereby declare it my new theme song. Clearly I'm a pervert.

Grabbing my cell, I sit on the edge of the bed and make the booty call. He answers on the second ring.

"It's been five days since I've seen you naked," he says with a serious tone. "Are you intentionally trying to kill me?"

"Do you think you could come over? I've already got my pants off."

His answer is to disconnect.

I kick off my shoes and strip off my pants but leave on my red thong. As I pass the mirror I fluff my hair and unbutton my shirt just far enough to show some lace.

By the time I get to the slider, he's jogging across the sand. He's without coat or shoes, even though it's fucking freezing. Not a minute was wasted getting his ass over here. I like watching when he doesn't know I'm looking. There's an awful lot to admire. The short-sleeved T-shirt showcasing his biceps and strong forearms is just one of them. Hubba hubba.

I think he's been lifting weights because they're bigger than a few months ago. And I believe he's healthier than those first days. The excessive drinking and the cigarettes both were taking a toll. The difference in his face and eyes is obvious. But within, where it really counts, must be renewed. Please God make it so.

He takes the steps two at a time. His cheeks are red with the cold and his nipples are hard. He looks up at me waiting and smiles. Thank you baby Jesus for this vision.

"Get your ass in here, it's freezing!" I say, opening the slider just enough for him to step inside.

He wraps his icy arms around me, drawing me against him.

"Oh! You're so cold!" I let out a squeal.

"Kiss me warm," he says, putting his icy nose against mine. Then his lips take the kiss.

Lord.

"Come with me." I crook my finger and head down the hallway.

"You're inviting me into the inner sanctum?"

"And into my shower. Would you like to wash my back?"

When I turn around he's already removed his shirt, and he's working on the pants. He sees my surprised expression and chuckles.

"It's been five long frustrating days and nights. You think it's easy going without you?"

There's no answer for that rhetorical question, but it feeds my soul. It's so powerful to feel the same. I could hardly stand not being with him.

He isn't wearing his boxer briefs today. And as his jeans slide down to reveal his already-hard cock I find myself biting my lip. We come together in an embrace. He takes my face and kisses me with meaning. This is no fast and furious run at each other.

I melt into the softness of his full lips and feel his hands move down my back. They land squarely on my ass, which is a great place to start. Pulling me against his body I feel him hard against me. He kisses my neck and his eyes travel south to the first button blocking his path.

"Let's get rid of this," he says, using his hands to take the offending shirt off. He drops it to the floor.

"My silk and laceable you." He smiles.

I reward the comment with a kiss.

"As much as I love the red, the lace, your hot body wearing it, there's nothing more beautiful than seeing you naked."

He takes both straps of my demi bra and slides them off my shoulders. It stays in place. His index fingers trace along the edges of the cups, and goosebumps rise on my skin.

"Let me see," he says softly.

I undo the back clasp and drop the bra. My nipples are erect, waiting for his mouth. He sucks on one then the other and runs his hands over my breasts like a sculptor feeling his masterpiece. It's almost reverent.

My fingers reach for his cock and I play with the length of him.

"Let's get in the shower," I say.

"Let's take off the thong."

I strip down to my birthday suit and the look on his face makes me giggle.

"I can't help it," he says grinning.

Then he picks me up in his arms and carries me into the bathroom. He sets me down gently and kisses my neck, right under my ear.

Opening the glass door, I turn the water on and test its temperature. He turns me back around to face him, and a kiss so perfect it should be taught in school passes between us. When our lips part I hear his soft moan. How wonderful a sound can be.

I step into the shower, toes flinching as they touch the cold tile floor. Back turned to the faucet thousands of warm drops trickle over my hair and down my back. A lively stream trails off my nipple, where Parish's eyes have settled.

He steps inside and puts his hands against the wall on either side of my body. Water washes over him. Wetting his hair, trailing down his face, even on his tongue as it follows the stream of water from my hair to my breast to the tip of my nipple.

I'll always remember this moment. The visual perfection. This ethereal state of mind.

Kissing his way to my lips in sweet slow motion, my body naturally arches against his. Here under the water, with the sunlight coming through the little window, I sense something. There, only visible in the distance. It's behind his eyes and hidden within the sound of his voice. It's in every small piece of him, and it begs for acknowledgment. But before I can put name to feeling, I get lost in his touch.

CHAPTER 11

PARISH

*E*yes closed, stretched out on the couch, I can't stop thinking about the state of things. Sometimes in life you can feel the shift as it happens. One day you're this version of yourself and the next someone you hardly recognize shows up. It's happening to me.

You hear people say good things come to those who wait. Maybe that's what's going on. My wait was so long and heart-breaking, the gods rewarded me with a woman like her. Because of Scarlett I feel like nothing is going to be the same anymore.

The writer in me tries to find the right words to describe what's occurred. I've whittled it down to two sentences. I was lost. She appeared.

But the realist in me isn't completely dead, and he's got a few questions. Where's this going? Could she bear my sorrow and hers? I shouldn't even be asking myself that when we've only just begun to know each other. Two and a half months is a ridicu-lously short amount of time to…to…to conclude how effortless it would be to love her.

I've been avoiding that word. On the other hand, it seems I'm only stating the obvious.

All these years and it's the first time I've cared enough about someone to look toward the future. Other than early relationships, the ones before I had a child, my heart has steered clear of attachments.

What I feel with her deserves a finer definition. Soul mate. I'm beginning to understand the concept.

This is new territory. And I'm a blind broken man traveling through. What do I have to offer when my emotional state requires so much attention? A man needs to be able to have a steady strength for his woman and be able to protect.

That last one I can do. It's the first part I'm worried about.

And then there's Sam. Just his piece of the puzzle is a lot to consider. First off, they're moving to Montana next year. I don't even have a full year. Maybe eight, nine months. If I want things to progress with Scarlett I need to know and want to take on the child. It wouldn't be right to build a deeper relationship with the boy only to have it lost. And who knows if she's even going to succeed in her new role?

Fuck. My head is throbbing with unending questions. I need an aspirin.

Eyes open to the dappled light streaming in the windows. The fog cleared while I dissected my life. If only my emotional mist would do the same.

A long sigh escapes as I rise, adjust my package, and head for the kitchen cupboard. While retrieving the Bayer bottle I look out the window. There's a group of boys walking along the shore toward the caves. I think Sam's among them. The red jacket's hard to miss.

Grabbing the binoculars from the timeworn rattan basket, I take a closer look. The stiff winds are making the boys hold their coats close. There's four of them, two older. Sam looks out of place. But it seems he's trying to fit in because one of the kids passes an e-cigarette to him and he takes a long unnatural pull. A steady stream of vapor trails from his mouth. It looks like it's never going to stop. Shit.

He's trying to walk like they do. I only notice because it's so unlike his own short steps. He hasn't had his first big spurt of growth. But he's trying on their lazy gait and long steps. All of them look like they studied at the same school populated with unimpressed teenagers. Devoid of energy or enthusiasm, life's tired them already.

A blurry figure passes quickly in front of my lenses. It's too close to see who, so I adjust the distance. Scarlett. She's trying to catch up with the boys and it looks like it was a spur-of-the-moment decision. Her coat's bunched in one of her hands. She didn't have time to put it on. Can't help noticing the bouncing boobs.

Without any thought, I put the binoculars down, grab my hoodie and head for the door. She may need my support. Grabbing my dark glasses and a handful of butterscotches I'm out within seconds.

I take the steps down to the sand and start for the retreating figure. The boys are almost around the jutting cliff.

"Scarlett!"

I try getting her attention, but between the roar of the sea and the howling wind there's no chance. Now that she's on the hard sand next to the crashing waves it's impossible.

When she gets close to disappearing from my view, I step up my pace. Just as she's about to make the turn I give it one more attempt.

"Scarlett!"

She hesitates then turns around to find me waving. It only takes a minute to catch up.

"Hey! Wait up," I say, taking the last few steps to her side.

"Oh good. I'm glad you saw me."

"What's going on?"

This frustrated expression passes over her face.

"I'm not sure but some fuckery is happening. Did you see the boys?"

"Yeah, I was watching through the binoculars. I haven't seen those kids before."

She starts walking and motions for me to follow.

"I want Sam back at the house. I don't know those boys and I told him he couldn't go."

I make the appropriate concerned face. "That's not good."

"I need to make a stand, otherwise he's gonna walk all over me for the rest of our lives."

"I'll be your backup in case he makes a run for it," I tease.

She gets serious. "It's not funny, Parish. I'm his protector now."

She's right. And I can see what a good one she's going to make.

We round the edge of the landmass and come face to face with the problem. Problems plural. The four boys stand in the entry to a shallow cove, lighting a blunt. Their flame protected by the rocky walls.

"Sam!" Scarlett yells over the ocean's roar.

All eyes turn toward us, but only Sam's look spooked. The other boys aren't bothered in the least, even though one of them is as young as Sam. These kids' faces tell a story. The adults don't hold any power over them.

Scarlett walks right up to the group without hesitation. I'm holding back a bit, just to show them who's in charge here. But Sam's eyes dart to me. Think he's embarrassed I'm seeing this whole scene.

"Get back to the house now," she says with zero room for disagreeing.

She's trying to lock eyes with Sam, but he keeps looking down.

"Let's go," says the oldest boy here.

Obviously he's the alpha because the other three follow his instructions.

Scarlett lets them skulk away, leaving their friend Sam to face consequences alone.

"We'll talk about this at home. I'm not gonna yell over this noise. Now get your ass back now."

Sam's grateful for the short reprieve. It shows all over his face. Now there's time to come up with his story. Who the boys are, why he did it, why the defiant attitude.

As we turn to start our trek back I see the tears in her eyes. I want so much to put my arms around her and comfort the raging-mother mindset. But that wouldn't work. Sam would bust us. So she and I talk instead, while Sam moves toward the house.

"It's okay. You handled that well. Separate him from the pack and make your wishes clear. Good job."

"I'm shaking," she says, showing me outstretched hands.

"Maybe you should regroup alone then tackle him face to face. Giving yourself time to formulate your response wouldn't hurt. Let me take him to my place. We'll say you're going to meet us there after you cool down. That's plausible. And not a bad plan."

"I guess. Okay."

"Let Sam worry about what's going to go down," I say. "Meanwhile, I can make sure he knows I back you."

The first smile I've seen today lights her face. I give her a private wink.

We walk the rest of the way in silence, I'm sure thinking of the problem from our own points of view. Sam's figuring a way out. I'm figuring a way to help. Scarlett's figuring how to communicate her authority, and mostly how a good parent disciplines. She's got the hardest job.

As we get closer to the houses, I catch up with Sam.

"Come to my place. Let her cool off."

He rolls the request around in his mind for a few seconds. That's all it takes for him to know it's his best option. I get a half-hearted nod.

She veers off in the direction of her place and Sam and I take my steps to the door. I lead, he follows.

"Want a Coke?" I say, walking in.

"I guess."

He plops himself in a chair and stares at me.

"That wasn't your smartest move," I say, talking to him like the friend I am.

"Whatever."

"No. Not whatever. That's what men with no opinion say."

Think I threw him with that comment. I bring him the Coke and take my place on the couch.

"Are those new friends?"

"What do you care?"

"I care because I understand what you don't. It's really easy to go off course in life."

He just sits with that for a moment. Then he hits me with the zinger.

"You did."

I pause for only a beat to let it settle. It wouldn't be right for him to see the wounded me.

"Exactly. I'm still paying for it. And I didn't have so-called friends encouraging me. It was easy enough to screw up my life on my own. I think you're a great guy, Sam. Don't want to see your sadness take you in the wrong direction."

"It was just a little weed."

"No, it wasn't. It was the open door."

"What does that mean?"

"It means I know how fucking easy it is to do whatever it takes to make your mind stop replaying dark thoughts. You can't bull-shit me, man. I know what I'm talking about."

"I don't see you stopping drinking," he says, not breaking eye contact.

His words hit me like a brick. It's true. My crutch is still being used whenever things get too rough.

"Well, I've got to work on that. But you've still got a chance to stop things before they start."

He hangs his head and I know I've said enough.

"That's all I have to contribute. Oh yeah, and your aunt is doing her best. Think about things from her angle. She lost a sister. She's hurting too. Don't be a dick."

When he looks up I'm smiling, hoping my humor will land in the right spot. Thankfully it does. He's grinning too.

Soft Break

I didn't anticipate spending my night as a one-man referee, witness of teen angst. I'd much rather Scarlett and I use the time more creatively. But my greater self knows the importance of what's happening here.

My part in the scene is small compared to the nervous woman and pissed off boy sitting at my table. It's all Scarlett and Sam's meeting of the minds. I'm just the buffer.

"When your aunt and I were teenagers things were a lot different," I say. "We didn't have social media or cell phones. It's a lot easier to make big mistakes now. And they stay with you. How long would it take for other kids to see the kind of friends you've picked? You can get pigeonholed and you haven't even figured out who you are yet."

"And in addition to that Sam, I'm inexperienced. I know grownups are supposed to have all the answers but that's not true. You're not the only one who feels like you're navigating a new world," Scarlett says.

"I know," he says, his voice softening.

"I hope so, because I need your patience."

Sam nods his agreement.

"And I promise to give you mine. It's such an honor being the person your mother and father trusted with their child. I need you to know how seriously I take it. Believe this, if I think you're in danger, hurting yourself, or engaging in harmful activities, I'm going to investigate."

"I know."

"If I notice big changes in your behavior, your grades, or see you isolating yourself from your good friends, I'm going to check it out. Because I love you, Sam, and that's why I'm so intent on protecting you."

Sam sits quietly. I'm certain Scarlett didn't expect an *I love you* in return.

"So, going forward I don't want you to spend time with those boys, or smoke weed. Those are nonnegotiable. Understand?"

"Yeah."

"I've spoken with Mrs. Clark and the principal. They told me about the incident in the hallway. I should have addressed it with you then. I'm sorry I didn't because maybe you would have known I have high standards. That won't be happening again, right?"

"No."

"Okay, good."

"And you should know your good friend Pete is sad you've dropped him. Think about it."

"Okay."

"We don't have to talk about this anymore. But I do want to ask you what you wish I could do or change, or any way I could help you get through this tough year."

He sits staring with a blank expression on his face. "I don't know."

I get an idea.

"Hey, I might have something that would help."

Scarlett's just happy she's not the only one talking.

"Great. What is it?"

My chair scrapes back from the table and I make my way to the closest shelf of books.

"It's something I've done since I was about ten. I did it this morning."

I take the blank journal off the short stack of them I always have available.

"It's more helpful than it sounds," I say, walking back to the table and taking my seat next to Scarlett. I slide the book across to Sam's hands.

"What's this?" He says it with his eyebrows knit together.

"It's a blank journal. You told me you used to like to write stories, right?"

"Yeah."

"Well, write yours."

Sam's eyes find mine.

"I know you've got a lot to say."

"I guess."

"You'll be surprised what you know about yourself. I still surprise myself every day."

"And that will be for your eyes only, Sam. I'll respect your privacy. I promise," says Scarlett.

He wraps his hand around the dark blue leather. Think that's a yes.

Scarlett's hand reaches under the table and repeatedly pokes my leg in excitement. But when I look at her face there's little beads of sweat on her upper lip.

CHAPTER 12

SCARLETT

The diner looks like something out of a movie. It's beat up. That's my best description. Old grey wood siding and a sign that has a missing letter. I wonder how long it's been that way. As we walk in, I feel Parish's hand on my back.

"Don't judge a book by its cover," he chuckles.

All eyes turn our way, like seeing a new customer is unusual. Or maybe it's seeing someone with Parish. I'm going with that.

"Let's sit over there," he says, pointing to the corner booth against the window.

As we pass the redheaded waitress she gives him a meaningful stare, smile, nod. But no words pass between them.

"I guess you've been here before," I say, sliding into the booth.

"Yeah. The food's good. Plus, it's close. When we have more time I'd like to take you to the city for dinner. Just the two of us."

"I love looking at your mouth when you talk," I say impulsively.

He gives me this dirty-boy look and a smile that makes my mind go in a new direction.

"I like looking at your mouth when you're sucking my dick," he whispers.

I throw a packet of Splenda at his head.

"You're the horniest man in America."

"Thank you for the title. I'll try to live up to the honor."

We amuse each other to no end. But the waitress is approaching, so we quiet.

"Welcome back, stranger. Now I see what you've been up to," she says, placing the menus before us.

When Parish pauses with an answer, she starts laughing.

"I'm just messin' with you, honey. Coffee?" she says, looking from his face to mine.

"For me, yes," I say.

"Me too. And this is Scarlett. Scarlett, meet Terri."

This seems to please her so much, she takes a seat next to Parish and pushes him over to make room. Oh, he's not going to like this. But when I look at his face it's not the reaction I expected. He's amused.

"This one's a regular. Two over easy eggs, beans, sliced tomatoes, and wheat toast. Easy on the butter," she recites.

"Come on, not every time. Quit exaggerating."

She rolls her eyes at his comments. I'm just enjoying the show.

"We both know who's telling the truth, don't we, honey?" she says.

"Well, now I'm required to order something different just to prove my point."

"Order whatever you like. I don't give a shit."

We all three chuckle at the declaration.

"That breakfast sounds good. I'll have what he's having," I say.

She gets up and adjusts her apron which is bunched in the fold of her stomach. Then her eyes lock on Parish's.

"I'm just happy to see you with a smile on your face."

Turning, she gives me a half smile and a wink. "Good for you."

With that she walks off to attend to the next table. Parish just watches for my reaction. I don't say a word. I'm not about to deny

I've affected his mood. I know he has mine. His slight series of nods confirms my opinion.

"I've been thinking. Well, wondering really," I say.

"What about?"

"There's pieces of your story I haven't heard. Important ones."

"I'm an open book for you. What do you want to know?"

This makes me so happy. He's not afraid of letting me in.

"Okay. First of all, who was Justin's mother and why did you have custody?"

I toss the question out like I'm asking about something much more inconsequential. But he doesn't flinch.

"Her name was Marsha. She was a regular in a club I used to go to. One drunken St. Patrick's Day we had sex. She got pregnant and when she told me I convinced her to have the baby."

"Whoa! You convinced her? That's unusual."

"I know. I was in my thirties and my mores had been well established by then. She was only twenty-two. I wasn't comfortable with the idea of abortion as odd as that sounds. Probably my catholic upbringing. I also didn't want the child to be adopted. I wanted the baby once I knew it could potentially not exist or not be part of my life."

"But what about her? Didn't she want shared custody?"

"This is where the story gets darker. My total lack of good sense when choosing a sexual partner came back to bite me in the ass. She wasn't mother material at all. I didn't know she took drugs regularly or smoked."

"Did she want to marry you?"

"God, no. She was a free spirit. I wanted to participate in the pregnancy as much as I could, but half the time she'd be gone for weeks, or just not keep me in the loop. When Justin was born with no physical issues it was the first time I exhaled."

"She just gave you custody?"

"Not at first. She tried to take on her new role, but it didn't suit her. It made me crazy. Legally she was happy to split the baby's time between us. That gave her time to party. But soon it was obvious she wasn't doing the basic things required to care for a child. And my time with him grew as she lost interest."

"How awful."

"It ended up with me getting full custody. Then Justin and I began the happy years. He was three."

I soak in the story and feel a new respect for Parish, born of his ability to standby his choices.

"What ever happened to her?"

He grinds his jaw and in hushed tones says, "We think she killed herself after the shooting."

Oh no. I'm taken aback and it's going to be a minute before I can respond. I feel my eyes filling with tears. For Parish.

"She overdosed. Not sure it was intentional but if it was I understand why."

My hand reaches across the table and takes his. He's fighting back tears too. At the most inopportune time our food arrives.

"Here you go," Terri says. But when she notices our mood she leaves without another word.

"So, now you know the whole story," he says.

"It's heartbreaking."

"That it is."

I let out a sigh and realize I've been mostly holding my breath. But I'll forge ahead. I need to see the entire picture.

"Tell me about your own family. Were they supportive?"

The corners of his mouth turn up. "They were spectacular. My mom and dad, my brother and sister, all of them helped and taught me what I needed to know. I didn't have a clue how to care for a baby or raise a child. In that respect you and I have something in common."

We start to pick at our food. But it's all show. I want to concentrate on his story and he wants it told. It seems cathartic in a way.

"I haven't seen any of them visiting you or even heard you refer to them. What's that about?"

He studies my face for a moment before he responds.

"Well, that's the other thing. Possibly my biggest mistake."

"Tell me."

"When Justin was killed I shut down. Emotionally, physically, spiritually. I went into such a deep depression there was no room for any other person. Not to help me or watch over me or anything. I didn't want to be around anyone. I felt like being alone in my sadness was the right thing to do to everyone else."

"Right?"

"Yeah. How can you be around people and see the sympathy on their faces? That's what would have happened, because I wasn't going to get out of my state. It seemed easier and more compassionate to sever the ties all together."

My mouth drops. "You cut off your entire family?"

"I did. My mother was already passed by then and my father was in the late stages of dementia. He hadn't known me for two years. I was able to support him financially from afar. He never knew I was gone."

"What about your siblings?"

"That's the thing. I walked away from them both. I couldn't find another way to cope except to hide. I know now it was wrong."

"This is the saddest story I've ever heard. And I know something about sad."

"But they never stopped trying to find me I guess. They called just a few weeks ago."

My lips curve into a smile. "Really? That's great. Did you speak to them?"

"I did. It was nice. Now the next time I'll call them."

"What're you waiting for? Hasn't it been long enough?"

He nibbles on his bottom lip. "Yeah, it has. I'm probably going to do it this week."

I squeeze his hand and my eyes burn with tears. "Do it today. You don't know how long you'll have the opportunity."

Scene Break

"Your grandparents are coming for a visit in January," I say to the curled figure in front of the TV.

Sam's head twists back. "Which ones?"

"Pop Pop and Nana."

His nose crinkles and he forces a smile. "Do they have to?"

I lay my knife down on the cutting board and move to the sink to wash my hands.

"Why don't you like them?"

"I like them."

"Then why the face?"

He gets up and comes into the kitchen. In a flash, two of my slices of cookie dough are missing.

"They're boring."

"Are they good to you?"

"Yes. They always want to talk to me."

"Is it their job to entertain you every minute?"

I'm throwing him with this.

"No."

"Then appreciate the fact they've loved you since the day you were born. Cut them some slack. They're almost eighty years old for God's sake."

I get zero response verbally. But his body language is speaking volumes. First his eyes study me, surveying the woman who just offered something to think about. Then the corners of his mouth lift just a little. So do mine.

He reaches for his journal, posed on the edge of the counter, gives me a nod and walks off toward his room. I wait the appropriate amount of time, making sure he can't hear my conversation, then reach for my cell. He answers on the first ring.

"Hello, beautiful." He says it so tenderly and sincerely it makes me swoon. It doesn't sound like he's ever said it before to any other woman.

"I just had to tell you about the awesome moment I had with Sam," I say in hushed tones.

"Can you come over and tell me in person?"

Ohhhhh. Can I?

"He's in his room. I want to! What shall I say?" I beg him to come up with something better than I can think of at this moment.

"Tell him I stepped on a sliver of glass and you need to get it out for me. And bring bandages to really sell the idea."

His lie is so effortless and believable it makes me laugh.

"What?" He's laughing too.

"You're a very accomplished liar," I say as I walk toward the hall closet.

"Necessity is the mother of invention."

"I'll be there in five," I say disconnecting.

I move fast. In a half minute I gather all my first aid supplies for the nonexistent injury and tuck them inside a tote. Now for my audition for my starring role in The Lying Aunt. As I walk down the hallway I'm silently practicing. The less I say the better.

"Sam. I'm going to Parish's. You going to be okay?" I say, knocking on the door.

"Yeah."

"Alright if you need me just call."

I don't wait for a response in case he suddenly gets the idea to come along. I make a hasty retreat out the door.

Taking my steps like I have wings on my feet, I spot Parish peeking around his porch. My heart races with the sight. The cold stings my cheeks and the ocean's mist settles on my skin, but I'm warmed by his sexy grin. And that face. Was there ever one so perfect?

We meet in the middle of his steps, hidden from anyone's view. I melt into his arms and the passion of our kiss. The moment is so powerful, emotionally and physically. The ideal coming together of urge and desire and destiny. He's the one.

My reverie is interrupted by his words. "Let's get inside."

As we make our way through the door, he takes my hand and brings it to his lips for a tender kiss. Our eyes settle in each other's gaze.

"How wonderful it is when you're here," he says softly. "It feels hopeful."

I press my lips together trying to hold tears back. He sees them glistening.

"Oh no. Are you going to cry again?" he says, kissing me on the head, the cheeks, my chin.

"If you kiss my lips, I'll stop," I say. "The one's down there. Or we can just talk. I did want to tell you about Sam's and my conversation."

His jaw tightens and a vein pops out on his neck.

"Get your ass in my bed, woman. Talking will come later. My mouth is going to be otherwise engaged."

Soft Break

Lying on my back, wearing one of his dress shirts, makes me feel sexy. It's probably not the shirt, but the fact I just enjoyed the most luscious sensations a girl could hope for. Parish has perfected the art of going down on a woman.

I'd like to think it's my inspiration but I never lie to myself. However he learned it, whatever series of ladies showed him the way, I thank from the bottom of my heart. Sisterhood at its finest.

He dangles a piece of apple above my mouth as he leans on an elbow. The fact he's still naked under the faux fur throw divides my attention. I take the bite.

"Now, tell me about your conversation with Sam."

I move a lock of hair from his forehead.

"It was so great. It wasn't so much what was said, but how we connected in the moment. His other grandparents are coming next month for a visit and he wasn't too excited."

"That sounds pretty normal."

"Yeah, but I felt inspired telling him to look at things from their perspective. And he really got it. I saw it in his eyes. It was a special moment. Then he went and wrote about it I think."

His eyes sparkle and the corners of his beautiful mouth turn up. "Did you feel like a mother?"

Then it hits me. That's exactly how it felt.

CHAPTER 13

PARISH

*D*amn. Finished chapter twenty-four. I'm churning out the latest novel in record time. That's funny. Churning has never been my aim. If someone else had said it I'd be insulted. But this collection of words that came so easily are good. They tell a great story. Probably the best of the series. Daniel Dustin, detective extraordinaire, meets a woman. Life-changing drama ensues. It's no mystery I mined that plot twist.

Haven't decided whether to kill her off in the next chapter though. It would be heartbreaking and life changing to him and add layers to the already interesting character. He would survive a changed man. Damaged but stronger. Those traits would be in the plus column.

But on the other hand, if the readers connect with her I could stretch the story to two or three books. It would be nice arc. Or they could stay together. She's interesting enough to hold her own against his darker moods. Her effect has already changed him internally, made him reflect more honestly about what he wants in life.

I close the laptop and stretch my arms and legs. Looking out at the sea I try not to remember how things were two-plus months

THE BEACH IN WINTER

ago. The Scarlett effect reaches deep. It's changed me on a level I wouldn't have believed.

The horror of my memories hasn't faded, it's just been reassigned to a place not so easily accessible. To feel happiness again is stunning. Didn't think it would ever happen.

And Sam. His influence is real as well. I've tried guarding myself against becoming tied emotionally. For now, I tell myself I'm happy being good friends. Because when they leave for Montana, which I knew from the start would be happening, it'll be difficult. I've already lost a child. And although it wouldn't be nearly the same, it would nonetheless be a hard loss.

I think a good game. But the kid's working his way inside. I catch myself missing him when he doesn't come with me on a walk. But that's getting more infrequent, because as time passes we can be found most days trudging across the sand solving the world's problems. Sometimes we walk and more often now we run. We enjoy each other's conversation and company. It's as simple as that.

The sea is putting on a dramatic December show. The waves are big today. Sunlight highlights their crests the way you see in oil paintings. Bet there's some good sea glass churned up and laid out for the taking.

I glance at the small wooden tray with the two red and one black samples. My meager collection of rare colored glass. Sam and I are always on the lookout. He's the one who encouraged me to collect them. I never would have copied what his father and he did. But turns out they never found reds or black in all their hunts. For some reason they've come to me.

My eyes dart to the cell lying on the coffee table. Quit stalling. It's much easier to go off on tangents of sea glass and writing than to make the call. My stomach is tight thinking about what I'm going to say. Be a man.

I roll my chair to the table and grab the phone. Wait. Let me call Scarlett first. I tap on her name.

"Good morning. Or is it afternoon?" she says, picking up quickly.

"Afternoon. Did you have a good conversation with Sam's teacher?"

"It went really well. He still needs to bring the grades up, but there's no other issues right now. And he and his friend Pete are talking again."

"Question. When exactly are his grandparents coming for their visit? "

"They'll be here in the middle of February. My family's coming for New Year's weekend. Why?"

"I'm going to call my sister and brother and invite them to stay a few days."

I can sense her unspoken excitement.

"Great. Have them come for New Year's."

"That's probably the only time they have off work. But I was thinking it's going to bite us in the ass. If everyone is here we have no place to escape to. You know for our extracurricular activities."

She starts giggling and I can picture her hand lifting to her lips like she does.

"Good thinking. But, on the other hand, we get it all done in one fell swoop. Hey, where are you putting your family?"

"Hotel rooms. There's no space here. Besides, I like my privacy."

"They're welcome to stay with us. There's an extra bedroom with two twins that never get used. I mean, if they'd be comfortable."

I roll the idea around for a few beats. She continues.

"We can say we're good friends and maybe I owe you because you've been helping Sam with his transition. I don't know, we can think of something."

"I believe you've graduated from the Parish Institute of Fast Fibs."

"I learned from the best," she chuckles.

"I don't think I'll go that route, but I'll think about it. It would be nice having them close. I imagine there's going to be a few long walks on the beach. I'll let you know."

"Cool."

"Hey, Sam's out of school today, right?"

"Yeah. He's in his room as usual. But guess what? Pete's coming over in an hour. I'm more excited than he is."

"Oh, okay. I was going to see if he wanted to take a walk to the lighthouse. I thought I saw some activity there yesterday."

"He'd love it. But can you wait till his friend shows up? You can go together."

"I can, but maybe they'll want to go it alone."

"Listen Parish, I heard Sam talking about you to this kid on his cell, and it was really sweet. He likes you so much."

There's a stupid smile on my face hearing her words. The kid likes me.

"Sure. That'll work. Have him call when they're ready to walk."

As soon as we disconnect, I find my brother's name and make the call. If I think about it at all I'll find an excuse to put it off. He answers on the first ring.

"Parish?"

"It's me. Surprised?"

"A little. You just cost me twenty dollars. Gayle made the smarter bet."

We chuckle and then there's a silent space.

"So, I was thinking maybe you could come for a short visit next month. Would you two be up for that?"

"Definitely...but we don't know where you live, brother." His voice breaks and trails off with the emotion of the moment.

I hear five years of sadness in his words, and one moment of joy. Fuck me.

Scene Break

I sit ass in the sand arms clasped around my knees, talking to the waves. Lately our conversation has taken an interesting turn.

The waves have begun to talk back. Set after set, they jump and crash against the shore in exclamation, throwing their foamy hats in the air. I like to imagine it's all in wild celebration of my change of mood. They're shocked as I am at the news.

"Parish!"

I look back to see the two boys approaching. The friend is a good two heads taller than Sam, and he's got thick red hair. There's an ease to their body language, as if they've traveled this beach and other paths together before.

"Hey," I say in man's universal tongue.

Rising, I brush sand from my hands.

Sam nods in his friend's direction. "This is Pete."

"Hi. I'm Parish," I say, lifting my chin. I head for the harder sand. "Come on, let's go down to the lighthouse. Have you been, Pete?"

"Yeah, but not in a long time."

The three of us take off into the stiff wind. It forces Sam and I to put up our hoods, and Pete to pull down his knit beanie.

"It's colder than a witch's tit," I say.

They start laughing. The century-old saying never fails to capture a new generation.

"That's a good one," Pete says.

Think I made a friend.

"You two both in eighth grade?"

"Yeah," Sam says.

"We met playing pony league baseball."

"You signing up this coming year?" Pete asks his friend.

"Nah."

I notice Pete doesn't challenge Sam's decision. I can.

"Why not? You over baseball?"

The answer doesn't come right away. I let the question sit till he's ready.

"My dad used to coach. They had to get another father," he says, looking out to sea.

"We don't like him that much," Pete adds.

"Oh. I get it. But man, you're going to have all kinds of coaches you don't exactly connect with. That's the nature of being on teams. If you like the sport more than you hate the coach, it usually works."

Pete hits him on his arm. "That's kinda what I said."

"You play, Pete?"

"Yeah. Second base."

"I was a catcher. Played in high school," I say.

"That's my position," Sam says, surprised at the coincidence.

"Hey, we could practice if you want sometime."

There's a grin on his face as he acknowledges my offer with a nod.

I leave the topic where it rests. Sam needs to come to his own conclusions. Sometimes it's enough to just put it out there.

"I read your book," he says.

"Good. What's that shit-eating grin for?"

"Nothin."

But despite his denial it turns to a laugh. A private joke between the two boys.

"I take it you enjoyed the scene in the library?" I say, knowing full well what a young boy would focus on.

"And at the beach," says Pete.

They glance at each other in a shared moment of understanding.

"What? Did you show it to Pete?" I say.

That does it. They can't hold back the laughs.

"That's a yes. Perverts," I say chuckling.

They love that one. Now we're just three guys walking on the beach, talking our favorite state of mind. Being horny.

"Any questions about anything you read?"

Pete's eyes go round, but Sam isn't thrown.

"He didn't use a condom."

Oh shit.

"Good catch. I should include that important step, but this is fiction. My character is never going to get a sexually transmitted disease. And it's not normally read by such young people, I thought I could get away with both the man and woman behaving irresponsibly."

"Oh."

"But it would be a really stupid thing to do in real life. Make sure you know that when the time comes."

I flash to the fact Scarlett and I haven't once used a condom. My vasectomy is only birth control. Rolling the dice is ridiculous at our age. But now that we've been skin on skin it would be hell giving it up. That's exactly what you never want young boys to hear you say.

"Are you clear about that, Sam? When the time comes in the distant future, make sure you act responsibly."

Now I'm embarrassing him. A flush is rising on his cheeks.

"I know," he says sharply.

"Tell me what you thought of the story. Did it hold your interest?"

"Yeah. It's my favorite book ever. I didn't expect the murderer to be the neighbor. I thought it was the brother."

"I'm glad you enjoyed it. That's what a good detective story should do. Make you look over here while the real action is taking place over there," I say, using my hands.

"I want to read it too," Pete says.

"You mean all the other chapters?"

"Yeah."

"You'll have to pass it by your parents," I say, wondering what I've started.

"Hey, I've got a question for you," Sam throws out.

"What?"

He locks eyes with me and goes serious.

"Do you like Aunt Scarlett?"

Oh balls.

"Sure I like her."

Both boys are watching me now.

"What?" I say, feigning ignorance.

"You like her in a different way I think."

What do I do? What do I do? To lie wouldn't do any of us any good. I make the only decision.

"Okay, you're right. I do like her in another way."

Sam elbows Pete in the arm. "I told you."

I hold my arm out and stop our march toward the lighthouse.

"Let's take a break. This conversation deserves our full attention."

I move to the berm rising to softer sand and take a seat. The boys join me.

"First of all, what do you think about it?" I say.

"I think she likes you too. Every time she's on the phone with you she starts giggling and playing with her hair."

Pete thinks that's extremely funny and goes off on a laughing jag. It makes me want to join him.

"I kind of like her giggle. You understand. It's a man thing."

"Ah huh," Sam says, digesting the information.

"Are you okay with the idea of us liking each other?" I say.

"I guess. How much do you like her? A little or a lot?"

"Not a little," I say, grinning at him.

In return he smiles his approval. Finally he relaxes into the conversation.

"What if we end up moving to Montana? Would you come too?" he says.

Here's where I need to handle things delicately. He's put a lot of thought into his questions.

"That's why we've kept things secret. Your happiness comes first. We thought if you knew you might be hurt if we ended our relationship or you moved. Your aunt is trying to make your life as stable as possible. Does that make sense?"

He nods his head a few times. And really, I think he completely understands.

"I'd be hurt too. I consider you a friend, Sam. And I don't have many."

"What happened to your friends from before you came here?"

Pete looks like he's watching the final game of the World Series.

"It's kind of a complicated story. Someday I'll tell you about it."

He gets my message. We need to be alone to have that conversation. Pete's been privy to enough.

"And the things we've talked about here, it's private information. Both of you. Make sure you keep it to yourselves. I want to talk with Scarlett first."

"You're gonna tell her I know?" Sam says wide-eyed.

"I am. When you care about someone you don't keep secrets like this. She should know that you know. And that Pete knows too."

"Okay."

"I won't say anything, Parish," Pete says, pretending to lock his lips with an imaginary key. "It's in the circle of trust."

"Come on, you two. Enough talking. Let's go check out the lighthouse."

CHAPTER 14

SCARLETT

*B*aggage claim sucks even under the best conditions. This scene is out of a horror story. Hundreds of people are laying on the floor, leaning against walls, lined up and fired up. Ready to lodge their complaints. A hundred and forty cancelled flights have ruined an already flawed system.

"Let's go out to the curb. He should be here in a few minutes. Where's your cap, Sam?"

Suddenly aware he's without the favorite knit cap my sister gave him, a look of panic sweeps his face. Shit. Please God, not today.

"Where is it!? I thought I stuffed it in my pocket," he says, furiously searching.

"Okay, we'll find it. You had it when we were at the gate. Check the outside pockets of the carryon."

His shoulders relax, and an expression of calm transforms his face.

"That's where it is. I remember now."

He unzips the luggage and takes out the beloved hat.

"Put it on. It's going to be freezing out there."

We maneuver through the anxious crowds. No, I've misidentified the mood. Pissed off is more like it. Everyone but Sam and I have just had their Christmas ruined. I've seen more mad faces than happy ones today.

Children are crying with boredom and impatience. Adults are attempting to retain their cool and the one ounce left of the spirit of the day. But for us a cancelled holiday flight is the gift of the season.

As we exit the terminal I notice Sam's expression.

"You're happy, right? It's all over your face," I say chuckling.

"You are too." He's as confidant in the statement as I am.

"I'm sure our family's disappointed. Everyone was looking forward to our visit."

"I told you I didn't want to celebrate any of the holidays. They all know too."

"They do, Sam. But I had to consider everybody. All they want is to support us."

We take our spot at arrival pickups, along the curb. The fact it's fucking freezing isn't the only negative. It's a madhouse of cars and taxis moving excruciatingly slow. Every ten seconds or so a horn blasts.

"He's probably stuck a mile back in this shit show," I say.

"I'll text him," Sam says, reaching into his pocket.

"Tell him we're in front of the statue."

There isn't much of a wait until the ping of his response.

"He says he's close."

"Oh good."

"And he says to look for a red Honda SUV."

"What? Wonder what happened to the Batmobile?"

"He was gonna rent something different for a week. See if he likes how it drives."

I look at Sam and realize the relationship he has with Parish is separate and independent of mine. I had no idea about the car or his plan. It's kind of cool that they have their own thing. That they talk about whatever. Man stuff. I think it's great.

"There he is!" Sam says pointing.

The red SUV pulls to the curb and Parish puts it in Park.

"Ho, ho, ho!" he says, getting out and coming around to the back.

He's dressed like Nanook of the North. Only his face is uncovered.

"Think you got enough on?" I say, my eyes taking in the head to toe look.

He doesn't answer at first, but just leans in for a chaste kiss.

Sam's already used to our small displays of attention. As soon as the jig was up we let him see. It's freeing.

"It's about to snow, and I may have to put chains on. Get in you two. I brought some jackets in case you couldn't get to yours."

"Thank you. Our luggage is somewhere lost in space. They're going to send it to the house."

"Welcome back, Sam. The last six hours have been boring without you guys."

"I never wanted to leave in the first place," Sam says, stating the obvious.

"It's horrible in there. Out here. What a mess," I say, sliding in the front seat.

There's already a line of cars waiting to take our spot by the time the three of us have buckled in.

"How do you like the SUV?" Sam says.

"I like it. Thinking seriously about selling the Batmobile."

"Oh man. I like that car. It's cool."

"You mean the bad paint job or the dent in the bumper?"

Sam laughs. I reach my hand across the center divide and entwine Parish's gloved fingers in mine.

"I'm hungry," Sam says.

"You just had a taco and a burrito in the airport!"

"That was an hour ago."

"Sorry. You're going to have to hold on. We need to get back before the storm hits," says Parish as we pull away from the curb.

Scene Break

"Holy shit it's snowing!" I blurt.

Warm inside our house, the scene outside stuns in its contradictions. It looks like Armageddon. Snow falling on sand is a strange sight. And the wind. I've never heard it so loud. In the distance, barely visible, is the dark raging sea.

"It's beautiful," Parish says, arms around my waist. "Like you."

"You mean out of control and cold?" I tease.

"No. Something rare and a little wild."

Sam returns from the bathroom just in time to see us snuggling. Although he ignores us, Parish releases his hold.

"So, what shall we do tonight?" I say.

"It may be Christmas Eve, but we aren't interested in celebrating," says Parish.

This makes Sam come alive.

"Finally someone listened!" He looks at me. "I know you were just trying to make Grandma and Grandpa feel better. Whatever."

"I'm onboard. I'll do whatever you two come up with. We can just watch a movie and eat a Lean Cuisine as far as I'm concerned."

Parish takes a seat on a barstool. "Let's not go completely goofy."

"What do you have in mind?" I say.

"This is the perfect chance to be creative. Use our imaginations. Right, Sam?" Parish says.

Sam didn't expect the ball to be thrown to him.

"I guess. I don't know!"

"I think we should have an opposite holiday."

Sam likes the idea before we've heard what the hell it is. "Yeah!"

"What's an opposite holiday?" I say.

"We'll take Christmas and its traditions and do the opposite. That can be our protest."

"Like what?" Sam says with over the top enthusiasm.

Parish gets up and starts pacing while he thinks.

"Let's see. Umm, well, there's usually Christmas carols. Instead we could sing rap songs. Or play jazz."

I watch as Sam becomes engaged in a way I haven't seen before. This is taking him out of his own head.

"Now you come up with something," Parish says to him.

"Okay. Umm, umm, I know! Instead wearing matching pajamas, we could wear each other's!"

Parish and I let that soak in for a moment then get on board.

"Good one! You've got the opposite holiday spirit now!" Parish says.

"We can draw names for who wears what," I add.

"Now you, Aunt Scarlett. Think of something."

Let's see. It comes to me quickly.

"Instead of giving presents we could take away something," I say.

It results in two confused expressions.

"Hear me out. We could each pick something we like that belongs to the other two. And we can steal it. That would be the opposite of having the Christmas spirit!"

I see Sam's excitement.

"And it can't be something big like a car, Sam."

"Shit," he says.

I'll let that one slide because he's so damn happy. I'm not going to sacrifice his few carefree moments just to make a point. Shit, I've come further than that.

"I've got a good one," says Parish. "This would be a perfect night to go camping. You know, like it's the middle of summer. In the living room of course. We can push the furniture to the walls and pitch our tent."

Sam's almost apoplectic at that one.

"Let's have hot dogs and s'mores!"

"Wait! How're we going to do that?" I say.

"This one needs a lesson in imagination," Parish says, pointing to me. His conspirator Sam nods his agreement.

Note to self...show Parish how wrong he is at a later date.

"What are we gonna have to eat besides the hot dogs? And can Parish make it?" Sam says with a sheepish grin.

Our laughter rises and takes up all the space in the room, pushing away any lingering sad thoughts. I know it's a temporary fix but I'll take it.

Soft Break

"How you two doing in there?"

Parish's voice carries from the pantry to the living room, where Sam and I are pitching our makeshift tent.

"Don't look!" I holler.

"Don't come in yet!" Sam adds.

"I'm not! Jesus, you've been at it for an hour. Dinner's almost ready. What're you building, the Taj Mahal?"

"We're using our imaginations."

I hear his chuckle. My comments hit their mark.

"Okay, let's get this over the top," I say, picking up the plum and orange beach throw we found in the linen closet. It's huge.

He takes the opposite edges and we hoist it over the ladder placed in the back of the space.

"Now we need to drape the two wing chairs. Oh, and no farting in the tent, Sam. Please."

He just laughs his rejection of my request. Why do boys find farting their favorite pastime?

When we finish it looks better than anticipated. It surprises us both. The back is elevated, and it sweeps down at the entry.

"Now put the tall lamps at each corner in front," I say. "And if the cords reach let's turn them on."

We've created a kind of Moroccan tent for the likes of Ali Baba and his harem. The area rugs we used inside sets the theme. Six battery-operated candles and my phone playing my new playlist sets the mood. I looked for theme music and found Shahrazad. Inspiring.

There's plenty of space for the three of us. The sleeping bags we retrieved from the garage are zipped open and ready for us to occupy. Because it seemed right, I placed mine and Parish's close together.

"It looks so cool," Sam says, crawling his way inside.

"Let me see," I say, following him on my hands and knees.

It's awesome. I've got to remember this when Parish and I are alone.

"Should we call the cook, to check it out?"

"Parish!" Sam yells loud enough to make me deaf.

We wait for his reaction like two kids who just stacked their first building blocks. His footsteps approach.

"Whoa!"

Peeking out the entry, Sam and I watch the reaction.

"Isn't it awesome?" I say.

"Awesomely awesome. Let me in."

He gets on all fours and joins us in our tent world.

"I love this. Very cozy," he says, stretching out on a sleeping bag.

"Peel me a grape, woman."

I exaggerate my laughter and wipe an imaginary tear from my eye.

"Stop! You're hysterical," I say.

"Isn't she part of our harem?" he asks Sam.

Completely ignoring our little show, Sam crawls out past us.

"I'm hungry. Let's eat."

He takes off for the kitchen, leaving Parish and I alone in Alibaba's lair. He rolls over on top of me.

"Stop! He's going to see us."

"Shut up and kiss me quick. We've got thirty seconds."

My hands lift to his face. "You always have the best ideas."

I give him the most heartfelt, luscious, tempting mother of a kiss. It's delivered softly and with a hint of tongue. The kind of kiss that can make a man hard.

When we part, he looks in my eyes and slowly shakes his head, side to side.

"What's that for?" I say softly, kissing his chin, cheek, and nose.

"When you smiled at me that first day, I wondered if I'd ever think of anything else."

My mouth automatically curves up.

"I guess nothing will be the same anymore," he says softly.

I'm not sure how to respond to the most wonderful thing a man's ever said to me. So I say what's in my heart.

"It's out of our hands now."

"Promise me you're mine," he whispers in my ear.

Chills travel straight to the soul of me. My fingers entwine in his hair.

"I'm yours."

Then Sam's voice breaks the magic. "Let's eat, people! I'm starving!"

I'm going to kill that kid.

Soft Break

"Whose idea was this, anyway? I look ridiculous!" I say, walking back into the living room.

Sam's pajamas are comical on me. The top is much too small across my boobs. I had to put on a sleeveless T-shirt underneath. The sleeves come halfway between my wrists and my elbows. The bottoms are too loose in the waist and too tight in the ass. The crotch too short and it's giving me camel toe.

Sam and Parish are laughing hysterically.

"Okay, don't forget your getup. You definitely win the prize, Parish."

Both Sam and I were waiting to see him in my nightwear, and it exceeded our expectations. I made sure to pick the most ridiculous outfit I could. The pink transparent long gown with fabric flowers at the shoulder straps. It was a gift from my own aunt who was an old woman when she gave it to me. But she knew what a young girl would like. I wore it so much two of the flowers went missing and the bright color faded to a blush. It's been in my lingerie drawer for years.

I've kept it because when I was fourteen I thought it was the sexiest thing I'd ever seen. It was womanly when I wasn't quite a woman yet. Now Parish wears it and I love it for a new reason. He's man enough to laugh at himself.

"Your turn, Sam," I say. "Parish, what do you wear to bed?"

I ask the question as if I don't know the answer. Parish smiles and Sam rolls his eyes. Don't think anyone is fooled.

"Well, Scarlett I don't wear anything to bed. Sam are you ready to go commando?"

A look of horror passes across Sam's face, but it morphs into an expression that tells me he's in on the joke.

"Ah, that's a big no! I'm gonna wear the outfit you always had on when you slept on the beach."

Shit.

He heads for his room. There's a shameful look behind Parish's eyes and I want to kiss it away.

"Well, he's right. Can't blame him for remembering," he says.

"Don't be upset. He doesn't realize what he said was hurtful."

"I'm not mad. Just so he doesn't come back carrying an empty bottle."

He waves off any further conversation about his past, and I adjust the seam cutting off the blood supply to my pussy.

I see the fresh look in Parish's eyes. He's not hating my get up.

"What? You like this look?" I say, happy to move on to other topics.

"I especially like the bottom half."

I peek down the hallway making sure Sam isn't about to pop back in. Then my hand moves to the offending seam. I take the waistband and tug at it gently. Just enough to spotlight my lips. I rub my middle finger over the fabric and feel for my clit. There she is.

Parish's eyes dart to the motherlode then back up. I saw his jaw tighten and the intake of air. Damn, man. I'd like to lay you down and ride you right now.

"Get over here," he whisper yells.

I take the four steps that seem more like four hundred. Looking over my shoulder, he keeps eyes on the hallway. But his hand. Oh God. It slides into the waistband of my bottoms and traces its way from belly to lips. It finds the offending seam and pulls it away. His finger ever so softly vibrates against my clit. His breathing becomes heavier like an animal that's about to devour the kill.

It's so hard to hold back the moan that begs release.

Footsteps bring us back to reality. Sam's coming. Parish pulls his hand away and I adjust my bottoms. We put a coffee table between us just in time.

"Ta da!" Sam says, entering the room with a leap.

Luckily, he has on a hoodie and running pants. He's barefoot and without a whiskey bottle. But the corker is he's drizzled some of my body lotion on his cheek, like the seagull has made a deposit.

All three of us break into fits of laughter.

"Nice. Very non-holiday of you," Parish says, his breath still slightly elevated, and not from laughing.

As he rises and walks past me toward the kitchen, I get a wink and a slap on my ass. Sam's taking it all in.

"Hey!" I say. "What did I do to deserve that?"

As he disappears around the wall he calls back. "It was just a love pat."

His words land in the center of my heart. And even though Sam has moved on to see what Parish has cooking in the kitchen, I'm stuck here. Staying steady in the glow of the moment. I heard the word love and nothing else.

CHAPTER 15

PARISH

"*I*'m getting too old for a sleeping in a bag," I say, getting up from the floor.

I run my fingers through a head of out-of-control hair and find a butterscotch wrapper hidden inside. Holding it up for Scarlett to see before it's stuffed in a pocket.

She blows me a kiss and gives me a little dance. "There's absolutely nothing old about you," she says, wrapping up the show with a twirl and a flash of her boobs.

"More, more," I say, smiling my plea.

The woman looks fucking hot. The baggy low-slung pajama bottoms she changed into this morning are deceptively innocent. The light-blue long sleeved top a little tight. It rides above the waistband of the bottoms and shows a sliver of skin. I like it exactly as is.

While she makes quick work of folding the tent linens, I'm returning the furniture to their rightful places. And thinking of the past twenty-four hours. Our non-holiday last night was a success. I keep going over about how much fun the three of us had together. We're a good team.

Ever since I woke up, the night's been replaying in my mind. I haven't been part of a fun family night in a long time. Not since Justin. He was always wrapped in the love of his grandparents and aunt and uncle and their families. Every holiday was a warm, loving scene.

That's what last night felt like, minus the traditions. It was rich with the spirit. All we wanted was for Sam to forget the holiday for a few hours. To take the sting of being without his mom and dad away for the few hours he was most likely to be missing them. That was our only aim. But we got a lot more in the bargain. Didn't know it would become something bigger.

A kind of a bonding happened. From my viewpoint anyway. There was an ease to our conversations and play. As if we'd been together for a long time, and this was just one of many memories we'd made over the years. It was so comfortable. Remarkable, really.

Coming back to the present, I check to make sure we're not about to be busted by Sam. The water's still running in the shower, so I've got a green light. I take the blanket from Scarlett and toss it on the couch. Then she's in my arms and we're dancing around the room to the John Legend song playing.

"How is it that you smell so good?"

I lift the long hair cascading down her back and put my lips against her neck. Kisses travel from ear to shoulder.

"I like this part of you. It turns me on."

"Everything turns you on. I'm not complaining, mind you."

Her hand takes ahold of my dick and moves to my balls.

"Did I jingle your balls?" She giggles when she says it.

"No. Can you do it now?"

Both of us are distracted by the sound of the bathroom door opening. Scarlett lets go of her handful of me. Damn. We stop the dancing and I adjust myself.

"I'm out!" Sam yells from the hall.

He was warning us in case we were getting crazy. How he

came up with that description we don't know. But he says it whenever he catches us being romantic.

"He's so funny," Scarlett laughs.

"Go along with me here," I say, taking her in my arms and bending her backwards in a Hollywood kiss stance.

She likes my idea. "Oh yeah! Let's freak him out."

I listen for the footsteps and when I know they're close I pretend to be kissing Scarlett like a man possessed. My back hides our faces, so I can really pour it on without actually touching her lips. For her part, she gives it her all, making little moans and loudly smacking her lips. It's disgustingly believable. I nearly start laughing. The reaction is immediate.

"Oh, nooo! That's crazy, you two! Stop!"

Sam continues with his review. There's yucks and fake hurls. It goes on until we decide to put him out of his misery. I turn our bodies, so he can see there's no actual making out going on. Scarlett pats my arm to stop the show.

"Get me up! My back!"

Sam's face relaxes. A grin replaces the grimace.

"Very funny," he says. "That was gross."

I take Scarlett's hand and we do a dramatic bow for the audience.

"Thank you," she says to an imaginary crowd. "We'll be signing autographs for those interested."

Sam shakes his head as he takes a seat on the couch.

"There's something seriously wrong with you guys."

But she and I are amused and reward ourselves with a kiss.

"God," Sam says under his breath.

I take a seat next to him while Scarlett continues with her blanket detail.

"It's still a non-holiday you know? Day two."

His eyes light up. "What are we doing today?"

"Well, there's still the non-carols and most important of all, the gift steals. We haven't done either of those."

"Oh, that's right! I've got to start thinking of what I'm going to take from you guys," Scarlett says.

"I'm gonna go last on that one. Can we do it right now?" says Sam.

I look at Scarlett and she nods and shrugs.

"Yeah, if you want. I'm sure we can come up with something," I say.

"Wait. How does this work? Do we steal from the other two? Or pick one?" Scarlett asks.

"The other two!" Sam hollers.

It surprises me that he's so adamant. But good. He's engaged.

"Okay, I'm going first," I say, watching the faces of my companions. "I already thought mine out."

"Uh oh," Scarlett says.

"Sam, I steal your cell for the rest of the day, so our non-holiday caroling will be uninterrupted. And Scarlett, I'll be taking possession of the red lipstick you wear. It looks great on you, but it takes me forever to get off my face. And my clothes. And my, whatever."

I'm happy with my choices, but I'm alone in the assessment. Sam's curling his lip, and Scarlett's eyes have gone wide.

"No! Not my Ruby Woo!!"

"Yep. Go get it and hand it over, wench."

"What about me?" Sam says. "You just lose a friggin lipstick. I'm giving up my phone."

I lean back and thread my fingers behind my head. "The king of the castle has spoken."

I get an immediate reaction from them.

"I'll crown you! This is my castle, you asshole," I holler.

"Yeah, what she said," Sam adds.

I just laugh. We all are.

"Sam, did you hear that? She called her king an asshole. I may have to chop off her head."

"Don't forget she still has a steal from you," he says.

144

Uh oh.

A beautifully evil expression comes over Scarlett's face.

"Thank you, Sam. I'd almost forgot. Let's see. What can I steal that would really make the self-crowned king cringe?"

"What about his old grey sweater?"

"No. That's not precious enough. Keep thinking."

Sam looks around the house and his eyes settle on the wrapper on the table.

"What about his butterscotch candy?"

My eyes go wide with fake horror. Scarlett's narrow in evil glee.

"That's it! I hereby steal your candy. From here on I'm in charge of your intake. If you want one you go through me. And it's for as long as you keep my lipstick."

Sam starts laughing and I know I'm screwed.

"Wait! I want to do yours over again. I should have taken all your lipsticks."

"Too bad. It has been decreed."

"You're really getting into this royals thing, aren't you, princess?"

"I'm the queen, not the princess."

God damn she's cute. Even when she steals my candy.

"What about me?" Sam says.

She walks to where he sits and plops down beside him. Her arms encircle his shoulders. He's feigning extreme discomfort, but I sense he kind of likes it. She kisses the top of his head.

"I'm stealing kisses. One a day."

"Noooo," Sam says, trying to push away.

But Scarlett holds strong.

"You can't refuse me. It's my choice. Besides, it's only one friggin' peck a day."

"I'm almost fourteen, Aunt Scarlett. We don't do that."

"Who's we?"

"Boys."

"Help me, Parish," she pleads.

I hold up both hands stopping any further involvement. I'm staying out of this fascinating conversation.

"You still have three and a half weeks till your birthday," she says. "Till then I want my kisses. At the very least hugs. I'll settle for that measly show of affection."

This makes Sam happy. He relaxes into her arms.

"Okay. Hugs it is. But just till January twenty-first."

With that he breaks away and stands in front of us.

"Now me. I know what I want." He says it with some embarrassment. This'll be interesting.

"I'm gonna steal an hour from each of you."

Scarlett and I look at each other, waiting for the other shoe to drop.

"That sounds easy enough," she says.

"I'm not finished. I want to go to Mass today. At St. Joseph's. It's the Christmas Mass and some of my friends will be there. What do you think?"

I don't think we could be more surprised about his choice of a steal. Out of all the things he could have taken from each of us, he asked for our time and company. And to go to church. Scarlett gets teary. The woman's a faucet.

"Oh, Sam! Yes. Of course."

She gets up and tries to embrace him again, but he moves out of her reach.

"Stop it!"

He laughs as he moves backwards toward the kitchen. Then he looks at me.

"Can't you control her?"

"You've got a lot to learn about women, Sam."

Scene Break

St. Joseph's is an old small church on the east end of town. Its rectory a house on the same property. I've been by here hundreds of times.

"How many priests stay here?" I say.

"Just three. I think."

I pull into the adjacent lot and park next to the church van.

The weather has turned, and the snow's melted. Even though the sun's out it's still cold. I grab my gloves from the pocket in the door.

"Okay, remember to silence your cells," Scarlett says.

"Parish has mine, remember?" Sam says, sarcasm heavy.

As we get out, I notice Sam scanning the full lot. He eyes every car.

He looks a little excited. For what I'm not sure. He sees these kids at school every day. It might be for the priest or the friends, but it doesn't make sense. Whatever. I'm just going along with his request because it shows he's beginning to heal.

As we walk up the few steps leading to the church doors, I notice him looking around for someone. Scarlett sees too. But neither of us question him. He obviously hasn't seen whoever it is he's looking for, because a minute ago I saw his shoulders sag and his mouth go crooked in a kind of frustration.

"You dip your fingers in the holy water and bless yourself," he says to me as we walk inside.

I don't tell him I know the routine. Or, that my family's catholic. Or that I went to private catholic schools for twelve years. And in a strange coincidence that my grammar school bore the same name as this one.

I don't want to get into the whole thing. I just give him a nod and let him take the lead.

The church looks beautifully familiar. Every church on Christmas Day takes on a special glow. I don't exactly know what it is, but you can feel it, sense it. Everyone looks like they're happy in a real way. Like they've just forgiven their enemy and been forgiven by someone they love. Like it's a fresh start.

Sam takes us closer to the front than I thought he would. We're practically at the first pew.

"Where do you want to sit, it's almost twelve. Mass is going to start," Scarlett says.

He's stopped scoping the congregation and his eyes have settled on just one. It's a young girl with long blonde hair and braces. And she's shyly smiling back at him.

"We are really dense. Do you see what I see?" Scarlett whispers.

"Come on," Sam says, leading the way into the pew behind where the cute girl sits with her family.

"Shhh. You're embarrassing me," Sam mumbles to us under his breath.

I look at Scarlett and see the tenderness in her eyes. We both know what's happening at the same time. This is how it feels to be the parent of a teenager.

CHAPTER 16

SCARLETT

hen I walk into the room I see Sam standing at the slider. He's got binoculars trained on something on the sand.

"What's so interesting?"

He answers without looking away. "Parish with his brother and sister."

A rush of adrenaline courses through my veins.

"Oh, give me. I want to see. They got here last night."

I make it to his side in two point two seconds and practically strangle him getting the cord off his neck. He makes a fake dramatic gurgling sound.

"Oh! Sorry. Let me look."

I adjust the focus and scan the scene.

"Shit. I can't find them!"

"They're coming back from the lighthouse. Look about a quarter of the way."

His instruction is perfect. There they are. Parish is wearing his camel pea coat and a knit scarf I've never seen before. He's smiling while the brown-haired animated woman next to him talks. Her hands and arms helping to tell a story that makes both men laugh.

She's pretty. Tallish. Thin. I like the white coat she's wearing. Every so often she affectionately touches Parish on the arm. I think it's just a natural gesture for her. Now she's linking hers around the crook of his. Her head tilts to his shoulder, and they walk together. He doesn't seem uncomfortable at all. That's a good sign.

I move to the brother. He looks a lot like Parish but a little shorter and a bit older. Very handsome. No surprise. There's a knit cap on his head. It's the one I found for Parish in the boutique in town. The brother's shyly smiling and letting the sister lead the conversation.

"What're they doin'?" Sam says.

"The sister's talking, and the guys are just listening."

"Sounds familiar."

"Smartass."

"It looks like everyone's getting along. They look relaxed in each other's company."

"I can't believe he hasn't talked to them in so long," Sam says.

I put the binoculars down.

"He told me you two talked about it, right? That it was his decision, not theirs?"

He sits on the floor and grabs the remote. The TV powers on. He mutes the sound and turns back to me.

"Yeah. He told me."

"Well, I don't think it was the best decision. But sometimes when you go through something so horrible, like he did, you don't think straight for a while."

"Hope they forgive him. I wish I had a brother or sister."

Oh my God. Sometimes he says something so tender it melts my heart. I start for him, planning to plant a kiss right on top of his adorable head. But his stiff arm and splayed fingers hold me back.

"Stop right there. You've already gone over your limit for the week."

And then, just like that, he makes me laugh.

"So, what's the plan? When everyone gets here are we gonna eat, play games, or what?" Sam says.

I look at my watch and realize I've only got another hour till they land. Soon the entire family will be here. We'll welcome in the New Year and Sam's upcoming birthday together.

"All of the above. Tonight we'll play some games. Your grandparents and uncles will be cooking. And Parish and his brother and sister will be joining us for both."

That last sentence gives me the butterflies.

"Good. I'm glad Parish will be here. Does everybody know you're boyfriend and girlfriend?"

I grit my teeth together and smile widely. "Not yet. But they will by the time he comes over. And let me do the telling."

"Shit! I wanted to."

He says it knowing I'm not going to object to his little swear on New Year's Eve. I've got bigger fish to fry.

Soft Break

"And so, long story short, we're together," I say to the gathered group in my kitchen.

I see exactly zero surprised faces staring back.

"Stunning development," Aargon says dryly.

"We knew you liked each other, Scarlett," says my mother.

"How?"

"You're the Queen of Tells," Noble says, heading for the dining room with a stack of dishes.

"The giggles and the hair twirling. You act like you're twelve when you do that. The night he came over to play cards, it was like you just saw Santa coming down the chimney," Aargon laughs.

"And he was just about to eat your cookies," Van adds.

"Very funny," I say.

But Sam thinks it is, despite the fact I'm not sure he knows what it means. He goes into a fit of laughter.

"You did not know. Not all of you anyway. Did you know, Dad?"

"Of course. You forget your father knows everything," he chuckles.

I see my mother roll her eyes. But she's smiling.

"I can believe Van figured it out. He's got that sixth sense," I add.

"Who do you think said it first," he says while opening the wine.

"What do you think about this whole thing, Sam? You like him?" Aargon asks.

Sam's gathering the silverware and handing it to his grandparents to carry to the table.

"I like him. He's nice. We go running on the beach on the weekends, and sometimes when I get home from school. And he's a good cook."

"Thank God for that. Otherwise you're doomed to eat your aunt's attempts," Nobel says.

The doorbell interrupts the Parish Report. Here we go. Butterflies take flight!

"And don't bust his balls too much, boys! Give the man a break," my mother says, all too aware of their MO.

The four of them talk at once, voicing fake assurances to go easy. Oh yeah, that'll happen. But what they don't know is I've got all the confidence that my man can handle whatever they dish out. I wouldn't be surprised if he doesn't give it right back.

My mother takes my hand and squeezes it before I head for the door.

This is it. Please let this go smoothly. Let his family like me. I open the door and the three of them stand bundled against the cold air. But they're smiling. Especially Parish, who locks eyes with me. I see another level of happiness in his expression. He's reclaimed the relationships, and he's just as shocked as I am that we've reached this point in ours.

"Welcome, and Happy New Year's Eve!" I say with open arms.
The sister comes right in for a hug, and I meet it with equal
enthusiasm. She squeezes me tightly.

"I'm Gayle. So nice to meet you, Scarlett."

"You too. Come in before you freeze your noses off."

As they enter the house Parish finishes the introductions.

"And this is John, my brother."

John doesn't hug me but removes his gloves and extends his
hand.

"Hi. We've heard such nice things about you."

"Have you been saying nice things about me?" I say to Parish.

"I may have mentioned a few things," he says, holding back a
smile.

The brother and sister are watching us like hawks.

"Let me take your coats. I want to introduce you to my family.
They're hiding in the kitchen. Parish isn't the only one who's been
talking."

I get big smiles and a nod from the sister as they remove their
layers.

"Sam!" I call, knowing everyone is trying to hear what's going
on in here.

"I want you to meet my nephew."

"He's a great kid," Parish says.

I take the coats to the closet at the entry to the kitchen and
begin hanging. Enter Sam, looking a little shy.

"And this is the notorious Sam," Parish says. "Sam, this is my
sister Gayle and my brother John."

"Hi," he says softly.

They don't go for hugs or handshakes. They tread lightly into
the new connection.

John speaks first. "Hi, Sam. Parish says you're his running
buddy."

That gets a smile but no words. So the sister gives it a shot.

"We went to the lighthouse today. My brother says you guys

have climbed those stairs a few times all the way to where it's closed. They're too scary for me."

"They're fun. One time we had a race up. I won," Sam says.

That was smart of her. Engage him with a topic a boy would connect with.

"I'm still not sure you won. It was actually more of a tie," Parish lies.

Now Sam becomes his real self, relaxing into the conversation.

"It was no tie. And you know it."

John and Gayle love the exchange. They're grinning and John pats Sam on the back.

"That's it, Sam. Don't let him change the facts. He used to try that with me when we were kids."

A voice from the kitchen interrupts.

"Are we going to have to stay in here all night? Come on!" hollers Van.

Muffled voices can be heard telling Van to shut the fuck up. But it breaks any last feeling of being uncomfortable.

"Let me introduce you to my crazy family. Come on."

I lead the way through the living room into the kitchen where the group stands pretending to act busy. It's not easy, because they've done the table setting in the dining room and the dishes are all prepared. But I catch my father rearranging the pickle plate and Aargon wiping an already clean goblet. The only ones not pretending are my mother and Van. They're taking it all in.

Welcoming smiles greet Parish and his siblings.

"Happy New Year!" my father calls as he walks to John and Gayle.

Each get bear hugs and kisses on their cheeks, which they accept graciously.

"Everyone, this is Gayle and John."

I make each introduction, going around the room. Parish is good at this. Better than I expected him to be. He's relaxed. So far so good.

"We're glad you're all going to be joining us for game night," my mother says. "And for the feast too. I hope you're hungry."

Soft Break

"I've never eaten so much! But it was delicious," Gayle says to her tablemates.

"Honey, that's because you haven't eaten French food like this. It's the most delicious food hands down," my father declares.

"The Mexicans and Italians might disagree," Van says.

"Not to mention the Greek and Japanese," my mother adds.

They both get a wave of my father's hand, dismissing their opinions.

"Let's play!" Sam pleads.

"Okay, so we're decided then. It's 'Who Did That?'" I say.

I hear three yays and get applause along with it. I focus on our guests who'll be playing for the first time.

"Okay, this is how it works. Pass out the cards, Sam," I say.

He slides two index cards across the table to each person except my dad. Noble passes out the pens.

"Dad has kindly volunteered to be the scorekeeper and host. So this is the premise of the game. Each of us will write down something we did in the past that would surprise the others. But you don't sign your name. Something like "I climbed Mt. Everest". Dad will read each card, hiding the handwriting, and we each guess and write down on the second card who we think it's about. Don't show anybody your guesses," I say.

"Or your confession," my mother says.

"And at the end we tell who said each one and who guessed right the most times," says Sam with an excited grin. "They win."

"Also who fooled the most people," my dad says. "There's two categories of wins."

"You've got to really dig for the worst or craziest thing you can remember doing," Van adds.

Parish and his siblings are already thinking. Gayle's eyes are lifted to the right and John's lips are pursed in contemplation. Parish is smirking with some memory. This will be interesting.

"Okay, I think we've got it," Parish says, nodding to John and Gayle.

My mother holds up a finger to take the floor. "Now, we don't know if Parish and his sister and brother will be at a disadvantage or an advantage. They don't know our personalities or habits, but that might work in their favor."

"How?" my father asks.

"Because we're all trying to trick each other," Aargon says.

"Well, we don't know theirs either," Van says.

"That's right. Shall we begin then?"

Pens ready, we wait for the signal. My father picks up his cloth napkin and dramatically drops it.

"Begin writing. You have one minute."

Nine pens start writing furiously. Everyone is trying to hide their card from their neighbor's prying eyes. The laughter starts almost at once.

"Quit looking, asshole!" Van yells at Nobel.

"I don't give a shit what you're writing. We've heard it all anyway."

"Yeah, you hooked up with your piano teacher, we know," Aargon laughs.

"Oh! Don't remind me!" our mother says.

Sam is the first to put down his pen. I'm still writing and so is Parish. His brother and sister finish almost simultaneously. Then Van, my mother, and Nobel. Aargon is next. Now it's just Parish and me.

Pens down.

My father rises and gives the final instruction. "Fold your cards in half. I'm coming around to collect them."

He takes the big silver bowl on the buffet and makes his way around the table. Each of us deposit our confession inside. He stirs as he gathers, mixing the cards thoroughly. Then he takes a seat at the head of the table and grabs his psychedelic-patterned reading glasses from the tray.

"Everybody ready?"

"Read on, my love," my mother calls across the length of the table. It gets her a loving smile.

Reaching in, he picks a card. He hides it inside the bowl as he reads.

"Number one. *I once stole a bikini from Target*," he says loudly.

Every Lyon hollers in unison, "Who did that?"

I look at Parish and then his siblings. "We say that after every confession."

They nod their understanding. And the looks on their faces tell me they're having as much fun with this as we do.

We all write our guess. I think that one was definitely Mom.

"Number two. *I recorded my father pissing. Then I played it for my friends.*"

That brings howls of laughter.

"Who did that?" we all call louder than the last time.

"Some freak," says Sam.

There's a few people who could have done that one. But it sounds exactly like Van. Everyone makes their choices.

"Number three. *I put both my hands on a nun's breasts in a conve*nt."

"Who did that?" We're going crazy, laughing, yelling our shock. Sam's having hysterics.

We write.

"Number four. *I almost got arrested for public indecency.*"

"Who did that?" We're getting louder and rowdier each time.

"I think we know who that's gonna be," my mother says, looking right at Van. He just raises his eyebrows.

"Number five. *As an adult, I purposely didn't shower for two weeks.*"

That one brings a lot of confused faces and one yuck.

"Who did that?" we say cringing.

"That sounds great," says Sam. "Wish I didn't have to every day."

His grandmother pipes in. "When you start liking girls you'll want to keep clean. Girls like that."

We write, and neither Parish nor I tell the others Sam's already at that stage.

"Number six. *I accidentally saw my parents having sex, and it made me piss myself.*"

Side-splitting laughter follows and general confusion over who would have that reaction.

"Who did that?" we yell to the heavens.

"Number seven. *I gave a Lyon sculpture away to a twelve-year-old girl.*"

Ohhhhh. "Who did that?" we say, all eyes darting to the artist.

"I'm coming for whichever one of you did that!" my father says, faking anger.

"Number eight. *I bit someone and blamed it on my best friend.*"

"Who did that?" we call.

"What a dick move. Must be Van," Aargon says.

"All of them can't be me!" he says.

We write.

"And number nine, the last confession. *I'm in love.*"

That one stops us all in our tracks. Oh shit. He didn't, did he?

"Who did that?" we say a lot quieter. It's followed by nervous laughter and too many eyes on me.

I can't look at Parish. I'm too afraid.

"And now for the scoring. Ready?" my father says.

"Oh, this is going to be good," Van chuckles.

"Number one. Who's the thief that stole the bikini? Please stand up."

All around the table eyes are on either my mother or myself. But it's Van who stands.

"What?!"

"How many got it right?" my father asks.

Only my mother raises a hand. "I know my children," she says. "Dammit, Mom. Now I won't get a perfect score! I was planning on fooling everyone."

"Why did you steal a bikini?" Sam asks.

"For a girl, Sam. It's always about a girl."

A mischievous grin shows up on his face. "I know. I'm number nine."

CHAPTER 17

PARISH

*S*am and I sit waiting for Scarlett to get dressed. Every afternoon it's the same routine, us twiddling our thumbs and her finding the perfect walking-on-the-beach outfit. She looks good to me in anything she puts on. I've told her a million times. But I don't deny I like how she always looks beautiful. I can't imagine ever getting used to that.

As of five minutes ago us guys have watched some *Animal Planet*, eaten too many pieces of fudge, and exhausted our usual topics of conversation. Just trying to fill the time.

"Your family must be back home by now?" I say.

"Yep. They left early this morning."

"My sister and brother did too. It was a good visit, huh?"

"Yeah, it was fun."

That's his three-word review of the holiday, his family's efforts and the laughs we all had together.

My mind goes to New Year's Eve and the game we played.

"So, now we know your Uncle Aargon recorded your grandfather taking a piss, your grandmother had a biting problem as a kid, and your Uncle Nobel skipped bathing because he thought it gave him a sexy grunge look. You've got a strange family," I tease.

"Me? Your brother touched a nun's boob."

I start laughing. "It was an accident. He tripped and ran into her. It's not like he copped a feel."

"Sure. That's his version of the story. What about your sister? She almost went to jail for running naked across the football field."

"You've got me there. Yeah, I guess you're right. They are weird. Except for me. My confession was mild compared to all the other freaks," I say with a straight face.

Sam pulls his head back in disbelief. "You threw up when you saw your mom and dad in bed."

"It was a little more than that, man. Plus, I was only five. All I saw was naked bodies doing weird things. It scared me."

Scarlett appears looking sweet as always. Love the leggings with the red stripe. She does a twirl for my benefit. I respond with a whistle.

"There's the girl who gave away her father's valuable sculpture."

"Said the man who couldn't stomach his parents kissing."

"Kissing? Well, there may have been some kissing involved. My mother's mouth was…"

"Parish! Be careful," she says, her eyes darting to Sam.

"I think that horse is out of the barn, woman. He's a teenager."

"I know all about it. My dad told me two years ago."

"See," I say, chuckling at Scarlett rolling her eyes.

"I think what we learned is that we're all messed up. Except for Sam here. He's just in love with his Amy."

The expression on Scarlett's face goes soft, tender. She tilts her head and looks at Sam like he's about the sweetest boy in the world.

"I'm sorry I said anything. You guys haven't stopped talking about it," he says. "I just wanted to win the fooling everyone part."

Scarlett gets that look on her face. The one that says she's about to try to get a Sam hug. He sees it too and gets up.

"I'm gonna cut you off pretty soon, Auntie. Stop it. And never do it around my friends."

Holding up her hands in surrender she says, "Okay, Okay. I'm stopping."

"Let's go. You finally ready?" I say.

As soon as the words leave my mouth her cell rings.

"I've got to take this. It's my friend calling from Montana. You guys go without me."

Sam and I both know this will be an hour conversation, easy. Scarlett's girlfriends have been supportive of her new life and call regularly.

"Let's go," I say, getting up.

Sam follows me to the door.

"Grab some candies," I whisper so Scarlett doesn't hear. I still have her lipstick.

He takes a handful and stuffs them in his sweatshirt pocket. I pull my hoodie from the hook by the slider and we head outside.

It's a perfect day. Bright sunlight, easy breezes and the churning sea. The waves are bigger than usual. But the best thing is the ocean's color. White foamy crests highlight the sapphire sea.

"Wow. It's awesome looking, right?" I say to the quickly departing Sam.

He's sprinting toward the shore.

"I bet there's some sea glass today!" he yells back.

Watching till he reaches the wet sand, I pick up my speed to catch up. Feels good to be running regularly now. My body's starting to feel like it used to. Giving up the booze is a big part of my return. It's happened so gradually I hardly knew I was quitting. One day I just realized I hadn't had a drink. I'm not saying anything about it to Scarlett. She's not much of a drinker and I doubt if she even noticed. Better to keep it quiet, in case I decide to have one some night.

Sam must have found some glass because he picks up something small and holds it up for me to see. Too small from here. By the time I get there he's stuffed another in his pants pocket.

"What'd you find, glass?"

"Yeah. A blue and a green," he says, pulling them out to show me.

"Nice."

"I'm looking for your reds," he says, head trained on the sand.

"Let's walk. We can look as we go."

"Then we can run back, right?"

"It's a plan."

We walk for a few minutes in silence. It's sort of our thing. We don't have to talk every minute. Makes things comfortable for both of us. Sam collects three more pieces, but all green. Then suddenly tosses them back to a wave.

"I've got enough of those," he says.

"So, your birthday's next week. What are you hoping you'll get?"

He keeps his eyes trained ahead and buries his fists in his pockets. Finding a candy he tosses one to me.

"Thanks. I forgot you had those."

"I don't really want anything. I'd rather forget the whole day."

I take his words in and think about how I'm going to respond.

"I hear ya. I want to skip the day after that," I say, unwrapping the candy.

His head turns toward me.

"Why?"

"That's my son's birthday."

Sam stops walking and takes a hard seat on the sand.

"Are we resting?" I say.

He nods and pats the spot next to him. "Yeah."

I use my foot to level the sand and then stretch out, leaning back on my elbows. He's sitting with arms clasped around bent knees.

"How old would your son be?"

That's all it takes to bring on the tears. My eyes are blurry already.

"He'd be fourteen this year."

"Same as me?"

I just nod and wipe a tear away.

"Do I remind you of him?"

"No, because I never knew him as a young man. I only knew the child. He was unique, and so are you."

He takes in my words, but remains silent.

"But it would have made me happy if he grew up to be as good a guy as you are. I'd have been proud to have a son like you."

His eyes fill with tears, mirroring mine. There are no words to accompany the emotion. But when he hangs his head and hides his face between his legs it says a hell of a lot.

I wipe away the last of mine and try to get my shit together. Then he speaks and I'm back to square one.

"I bet you were a good father."

"Thank you, Sam. I loved him. I always will."

The tears come hard now. Harder than they ever have before. What's happening? I can't control them. I stand up and start pacing, not really knowing where to go or what to say. It's just all coming out. The grief, the horror, the stark realization nothing I do can change the fate of my child. And here amidst it all the truth comes to me. I can't continue to live inside the pain forever.

In the moment it's as if I'm watching myself from above. I'm aware snot is dripping from my nose and I hear the sobbing. I can't take another step, so I kneel in the sand and sit on my legs. If I could I'd curl into a ball and roll into the ocean.

That's when I feel Sam move right beside me. Arms go around my shoulders and his head leans against mine.

"It's okay. Just let it out. I'll be sad with you."

And so I do. Unrestrained and void of any thought other than my boy. And Sam lets go too, crying for his lost parents. Knowing he'll never see them again.

"I miss them so much," he whisper sobs in my ear.

A kind of beautiful thing happens. Hearing the suffering of a child brings me back to earth. I begin to get in control of my emotions. This is where I'm needed right now. Sam's wound is fresher and he's barely fourteen. Justin would want me to help. Even at eight he was a kind boy. So, in honor of Justin I console Sam.

"Hey. It really sucks, doesn't it?" I say it between sobs. "But we can help each other cope. When you're down I want you to call me or come over. We can go for a run, or a yogurt or something. Whatever you want we'll do. We can survive our sorrows together."

He sits up.

"I was doing better but then Christmas and New Year's. And now my birthday," he says, shaking his head and wiping his nose.

"Listen, I hated every holiday till I met you and your aunt. Every single one. But it's changing. I feel it. You guys are healing me in some way. And I thank you for that. Just be patient with yourself, Sam. It's not going to happen overnight."

He looks in my eyes and gives me a half smile. Just to show he's heard.

"Remember one thing. When you've loved someone as much as we did, your grief is big. But I'd rather of had the love. The kind most people miss out on. Wouldn't you?"

"Yeah. For sure," he says, sniffing his tears to a stop.

"What we have is the memories of being alive together. I'm going to hold on to those."

"Me too."

Before another word passes between us LK's new Golden Retriever, Geronimo barrels into us. He's wet and covered in sand. It breaks our thoughts of death and loss. This is life. At the same time a green tennis ball sails over our heads and lands a foot behind where we sit. The dog is blissfully unaware he just mowed down two people as he goes for the prize.

"I'm sorry! Oh, you alright?"

The lighthouse keeper walks up and offers Sam a hand. He carries the dog's leash. Poor guy. He wears a horrified look on his face.

"I overshot my target," he says. "Again, I'm so sorry."

Sam stands and brushes the sand from his pants. I do the same. The dog brings the tennis ball back to the scene of the crime and offers it to Sam. The man has noticed we've both been crying. How could he miss it?

"We're okay," I say. "No worries."

"Can I throw the ball?" Sam asks.

"Sure. He'd love it."

Sam throws it as hard as he can. It sails across the wet sand and lands at the edge of the sea. For a few beats it's lost in the foamy edge. Dog and boy take off.

"I've seen you out here giving Geronimo fetching lessons."

He laughs. "He's got that down pat. It's all the other things I'm having trouble with, like potty training."

"Oh, that doesn't sound good."

"It's a literal shitshow in the house. But, I do know, it's good having a dog's company."

"Yeah. I get it."

"I'd better try and catch up with those two young fellas."

He turns and starts for his dog, who's running in and out of the waves that roll to the shore. Sam's giving him a workout. Youthful dogs and people are a good match.

"Have a good day," LK says with a wave of his hand.

I stand watching the scene. Sam has done a complete turn-around. No more tears. There's a big smile on his face and he's never looked happier since we met. It's the dog.

As I start walking toward them I'm formulating a plan. Now I just need to sell it to Scarlett.

CHAPTER 18

SCARLETT

*F*resh snow lines the highway as we drive toward Winterfest. The first I heard of it was a few days ago. Portland, Maine's festival is famous apparently. I've got to thank Parish for the idea. Sam didn't hesitate when we offered to spend his birthday weekend there. He got more excited than I knew he would.

"How much longer?" he says from the backseat.

He's furiously texting. Responding to someone who's doing the same.

"I think it's only a few more miles. We've got to check into our hotel and then we can walk to the festival," Parish answers.

"Are you excited?" I say, turning to face Sam.

He looks like he is, sitting in the center seat watching for our turnoff.

"I want to go sledding first. Then can we go skating? Or wait. Maybe we can see when the hot wing eating contest is."

"Whatever you want. It's your birthday. We're going to do it all. Even your aunt's going to participate."

I give Parish an *oh no you didn't* look. "What's that supposed to mean?"

Sam starts chuckling and Parish follows.

"It means I paid attention when you told me about your coordination problem. Maybe ice skating isn't in your wheelhouse. I'd hate if you broke a leg putting on an ice skate."

Then he looks in the backseat mirror. "Am I right, Sam?"

"I think she'd fall on her butt. I can just picture it now," he laughs.

I feign anger. "I'm insulted! I'll have you both know I was an excellent rollerblade skater back in the day."

"Maybe in the olden days," Sam mumbles under his breath.

"And rollerblades aren't ice skates. Two very different things," Parish adds.

"Besides, I've done more exciting things than you two put together. I've zip-lined in Machu Pichu. I've gone white water rafting in Tennessee. Just to name a few. I've ridden a camel in Bethlehem for God's sake. What exactly makes you guys think I'm not the adventurous type?"

They burst out in laughter as if it's so obvious they don't need to explain.

"You two assholes!" I say and mean.

Now all three of us are laughing. I don't mind that it's at my expense. All I care about is giving this beautiful boy a good birthday.

"There's the turnoff. A quarter mile."

He gets in the right-hand lane and takes the Downtown Portland ramp. It looks like a winter wonderland. We go less than a block.

"There it is," I say, pointing to the Fireside Suites sign.

"All right."

He turns into the driveway and pulls under the covered entry. My cell rings.

"I'll go and check in. Be back in a minute," he says.

"I'm going too," Sam says, sliding out and hurrying to accompany Parish.

I nod my agreement and take my mother's call.

"Hi, Mom."

"Hello, darling. Are you in the car? Our connection isn't the best."

"Yeah. We're in Portland for the weekend for Sam's birthday. There's a winter festival."

"Oh, that sounds nice. Is Parish with you?"

"Yes, Mom," I say with a smile on my face. I know the news makes her happy.

"That man has a good heart. I mean, he and Sam seem to genuinely like each other. I'm so glad because I think that's helped both of you."

"Listen to what he did. The festival was his idea and he went and bought each of us backpacks and filled them with the equipment we'd need to have. Like ice skates and hand warmers, gloves. I haven't seen everything yet, but isn't that awesome?"

"What a kind thing to do. It's impressive, Scarlett. Wait till I tell your father."

"Oh, here he comes, Mom. We've got to check in. I'll call you tomorrow. Okay?"

"Yeah, that's fine. Give Sam a kiss from us and we'll sing him happy birthday tomorrow on his big day."

"That's good. Bye, Mom."

I disconnect just as the boys get back inside.

"Wow! It's freezing. I should have put on my coat," says Parish.

I take his cold hands in mine and try to warm them.

"We got a suite, Auntie. It even has a fireplace."

"It does? That's awesome."

He starts the car and we head for the far side of the building.

"We have two queen beds," Parish says. "I thought it would be more fun if we were all together."

When our eyes meet a silent agreement passes between us. He sacrificed sex for Sam's benefit. Gave up any hope for private time. But wow. It's about the most romantic thing he could have done.

Amazing. This is a kind of romance I didn't know existed. One that has nothing to do with loving words or bouquets of beautiful flowers. It's more meaningful. I feel like he not only did it for Sam, but for me. He knew I'd feel funny having him stay alone in a strange room on his birthday. Especially this first one without his parents.

So Parish put us first. Without making Sam feel uncomfortable and ahead of his own desires. It makes me love him more than ever. I mean want. It makes me *want* him more than ever.

Scene Break

Standing at the entry downtown builds our excitement. There's winter revelers on every corner and strolling down the middle of the street. Each venue has a line forming. Snowmen and snowflake decorations adorn windows of the shops and restaurants. I've seen *Frozen* references everywhere and little girls dressed in character.

We're bundled against the cold. Knit caps, thick gloves, down jackets. Parish looks fucking sexy. There I said it. I know I'm not supposed to think of his cock this weekend but that's like asking the magnolias not to blossom. *Not going to happen.*

Sam's surveying the scene. It's his stealth mode.

"Who're you looking for?"

"No one. Just looking around."

"Okay here's what we need to do," Parish says, reading the *Winterfest Guide*. "We should sled and ice skate first, before the hot wing eating contest. We don't want to throw up going downhill."

"Are you both entering that? You're crazy."

Two voices answer with fists pumping. "Wings! Wings! Wings!"

"I'll cheer you on and hold your heads later when you're barfing."

Parish waves my concerns off and continues laying out our itinerary. "After that we can do the horse-pulled wagon ride."

"That sounds good," Sam says enthusiastically. "I want to see the ice carvings too."

"What about food? Hot wings aside," I say.

"There's a whole street with all kinds of food. There's a chili chowder booth and s'mores. I saw food trucks lined up for an entire block."

"Come on!" Sam calls out, already five steps ahead.

We follow him to the bottom of the hill. Plows have pushed the fresh snow to form a high slope. A banner proclaiming Sledding Hill spans the width of the run, and families stand waiting their turn.

"There's where we get the sleds," Parish says pointing. "Get in line with Sam. I'll get our sled."

Walking through the crowd makes me wonder if my nose is as red as the ones I see. Vapor rises from the mouths of happy laughing children.

"Ready to ride?" I put an arm around Sam and just as quickly remove it. I'm always forgetting rule number two.

"Yeah. You coming?" he says.

"Absolutely. I'm a badass, Sam. This little hill doesn't scare me," I tease.

"Auntie, it's bigger than it looks. Wait till you look down."

I wave his concerns away as Parish approaches.

"That thing's huge!" I say, admiring the long sled.

He mouths the words 'That's what she said' so only I can see.

I poke him in the arm, but the jacket's so thick he probably doesn't feel a thing.

"Are we all going together?" Sam asks.

"Of course."

"I want to be in the front!"

"You'll get on first, then your aunt, and I'll bring up the rear."

The line moves quickly as people take their place at the top of the hill and push off. The closer we get the higher it seems.

"I told you," Sam says, noticing my new look of panic.

Parish puts an arm around me as we make it to the top.

"I'll hold on to you. You're going to love it."

A weird sound escapes me. It's like a wounded animal.

"I don't know. You two could go together and I'll just walk down."

"Come on, Auntie!" Sam says as he climbs aboard the sled.

People are starting to look aggravated at my hesitation. Shit. Parish takes my hand and guides me to my spot behind Sam. Shit. I straddle the death trap and take a hard seat.

"Okay, Good. Now me," Parish says, taking his place without hesitation.

Now I'm trapped. His legs and arms surround me and I hear nervous laughter coming from my own mouth. Here we go. Shit!

I'm not sure how we launched but I think it was Parish pushing off with his hands. Oh Gooooooood!

It's fast. It's so fucking fast. Picking up speed by the second. Cold wind bites my face and steals my breath. Parish holds me tight and I'm sure I'm cutting off Sam's circulation with my locked legs. But it's exhilarating. Yeah!

By the time we slide to solid ground and pass the finish line, I'm starting to enjoy the experience.

"Wheee!"

"See! I told you," Sam says, turning his face to me.

We glide to a stop.

"Everybody off!" Parish says, getting upright first.

"Let's do it again!" I say loudly.

The two of them return my enthusiasm. We get back in line.

After three more runs we decide to move on, because there's only one day to fit everything in. Tomorrow's for something much different.

"We better do the hot wing contest. I don't think there's

enough time to get our ice skating in before one o'clock," Parish says.

"Hey, trade beanies with me," Sam says, eyeing Parish's OPI surf hat.

"This is old. You like it better than your new one?"

"Yeah. Is that okay?"

Parish removes the hat and tosses it to Sam. The hats are exchanged and Sam looks happy with his choice. I'm thinking there's more to this. Who's he trying to impress? I don't know. Maybe I'm completely off.

"There's the tent. Let's get signed up," Parish says.

We walk across the street and to the white tent set up in the parking lot of the Chicken House Restaurant. A sign up table greets us when we enter, and Sam writes in his and Parish's names for the second round of the contest.

Already the first group is sitting at the two long tables. There's a narrow space between them where a man with a timer stands pacing. The three of us take our seats with all the other second rounders waiting against the tent walls.

"All right, contestants," the host begins. "On my signal you'll begin. You must clean all the chicken off the bones. No half-chewed wings. There's a water bottle in front of each of you. Because these are The Chicken House's famous, or more accurately infamous, hot wings. Last warning. You can back out now," he says dramatically. "Everyone ready?"

"Oh, you guys are going to regret this," I whisper to Parish.

"Alright, begin!"

The tables of wing lovers start chomping. The three women that entered are just as messy minded as the men and boys. Already I see the reactions to the hot sauce marinade. Within a minute one man has dropped out. But it doesn't stop the others.

All of us on the sidelines are cheering our favorites on. Parish likes the older woman who looks like she may have a chance at winning. Her pile of bones is higher than the others. I don't really have a favorite so I just clap my hands with the rest of the crowd.

But Sam. When I turn to say something to him he's staring at the entry. And he's wearing a shy smile. My eyes follow his gaze. There stands his "girlfriend" Amy. Looks like she's with her family. I recognize her father from church, and the two brothers.

"There's Amy!" I say, knowing the information isn't new to him.

"I know. She told me they might come."

Parish hears our comments and takes a look.

"Go say hi," he says.

Sam hesitates and looks like it was just proposed he speak before Congress.

"Tell her you're going to be in the next contest," says Parish softly.

Sam rises and stands steady for a few beats. It's like he's glued to the floor.

"Go," I say. "And say hello to the father too."

With an intake of breath, he walks over to the girl. We don't want to stare or make it look like we're watching, but we are. Words are exchanged but we can't hear them. There's smiles all around except for the older brother who isn't paying attention.

The girl is just as happy to see Sam as he is her. It passes through my mind that she's who he was texting. They probably knew they'd see each other. Yep. That's how I would have played it.

"She's a cute girl. Watch how he looks at her," Parish whispers.

Oh God, it's adorable. Young love is the sweetest.

While we were distracted, the contestants have piled up the carnage of their feast. The older woman's arms raise in the air.

"We have a winner!" The announcer clicks the stopwatch. "Darlene Baker is the winner of round one! Again I might say!"

Applause breaks out, followed by whistles and loud conversations.

"As soon as we clear the tables, the second round will commence. The time to beat is three minutes thirty-three seconds."

I pat Parish on the back. "Good luck!"

His smile tells me he has no doubts about his abilities. Walking up to Sam he says something to the group and offers his hand to the father. Nice. Then I watch as Parish, Sam, the father, and the oldest brother take seats at the cleared table. I catch Amy's eye and wave her over.

"Hi, Amy! Here, sit here," I say, patting the empty seat next to me.

"Hi, Mrs., Miss."

"Call me Scarlett."

Her sweet face and blonde hair almost look angelic. But I'm sure that's not how Sam sees things.

"Who do you think's gonna win?" I say.

"My father wins every year. But I hope it's Sam," she says, lowering her eyes.

"Me too. Parish and Sam have never eaten these before. Are they super hot?"

Her jaw drops. "Oh no. They're gonna be surprised. They're too hot for most people."

The announcer goes through the same spiel he gave the first group. Then holds up his stopwatch.

"Contestants, begin!"

It's fair to say Parish's eyes started tearing up with the first bite.

Scene Break

"Scarlett! Bring me some more Maalox. And leave it outside the door. Don't come in!"

I have no intention of entering. But I can't help but laugh at the situation we're in. He's been in the bathroom since we got back, and the sounds coming from inside can't be unheard.

I've been holding back my laughter for an hour. If he knew just how good the acoustics are in this suite he'd kill himself.

I place the Maalox on the floor by the door. "Can I bring you something to drink? Water?"

"No! Go away! Please! Oh shit."

I chuckle as I walk away to the melodic sounds of the season. My cell sounds.

"Hi," I say, happy it's Sam calling.

"Hi. I'm checking in like you told me. We're all going to dinner. Is that okay?"

"Mr. Casper too? Are Amy's brothers going?" I say.

"Everybody. Her mom finally got here too. We're all going for chili and if it's alright we're gonna watch the nighttime ski and snowboard parade. There's fireworks after too."

"Will they be able to bring you back here?"

"Yes. They already said that," he says, impatient to get off the phone.

"Have a good time, and do you have enough money to treat Amy to something?"

"Yeah. Parish gave me a twenty."

"Okay. Have fun, birthday boy. Auntie loves you."

CHAPTER 19

PARISH

"*W*here're we going?" Sam asks from the backseat. "My birthday was yesterday."

I'm doing pretty good at handling the fact it's Justin's. Distraction is the way through.

"Yesterday was your present from Parish. Today it's my turn to dazzle you," Scarlett says.

She's as excited as Sam is, maybe more. Because she knows what this will mean to him. We've kept it under wraps. A birthday gift this good should be milked.

"You're going to love it," she says.

"Are we almost there? How long do I have to wear this?" Sam says.

I watch him through the backseat mirror, adjusting the blindfold.

"Don't peek! You'll ruin the surprise," I say.

He sighs in resignation. "Give me one hint."

"Okay. Let's see. Help me, Parish."

"Your present is one-of-a-kind. Right, Scarlett?"

"True. And that's a great clue." She touches my arm.

Sam sighs his frustration. "That's a shitty clue."

"No it isn't. How many things are one of a kind? Can you think of any?"

He mulls things over. "Then it's not clothes, or sports equipment."

"Nope."

"It can't be music or movies or technology. Man, this is hard. Give me another clue."

"We're here," I say.

Turning into the lot we park right in front of the entry. That was just good luck. Now when we do the big reveal it'll be more dramatic. The Portland Animal Rescue sign is right in front of the car.

But before we can do that the sound of dogs barking carries from inside the building to where we sit.

I turn to watch his first sign of recognition. Sam tilts his head, angling toward the sound. A smile lifts the corners of his mouth.

"Go ahead, take it off," Scarlett says excitedly.

He rips it away and sees where we are, reading the sign.

"Oh God, oh God, oh God!" he says.

We're all three about to burst. Then his eyes fill with tears, followed by ours.

"Am I getting a dog?"

He's stunned. Like never in his wildest dreams did he imagine it would happen.

"Yes! It was Parish's idea," she says, giving credit where due.

His expression is mature gratitude mixed with the wonder of a boy. This is the best thing we could have done. My hard won wisdom has taught me all about making the small moments count.

Sam's out of the car before we've unfastened our seatbelts. He runs inside with us hurrying to catch up. I grab the leash I bought last week from the back of the car and come around to meet Scarlett.

The double glass doors shut behind him, then open at our approach.

He's at the front desk, telling the tech he's here to choose a dog. We join them. Her name badge reads Dolly.

"Hello," Scarlett says. "We called this morning. I'm Scarlett Lyon and this is Sam," she says, putting a hand on his shoulder.

"Wonderful," says Dolly. "Let me take you back to the kennels. Unfortunately, we have too many beautiful dogs here. You're sure to find one to love. Ready to meet your new best friend, Sam?"

He just nods his answer. I think he's too overwhelmed to put words to feelings.

Dolly takes us through another door and down a hall, past closed-door rooms on either side. The sound of excited canines gets louder and louder as we approach one final door.

"Take your time and I'll be following behind to answer any questions."

We pass through the door and are greeted by dogs of all kinds. Each has its own kennel and its own personality. Some are doing all they can to get our attention. I don't know where to look first, which dog to offer affection to. So I just go from one to the other.

Sam and Scarlett are doing the same, scratching an ear or talking baby talk to a sweet face.

"What's this guy's story?" Scarlett asks.

Dolly walks up and looks in the cage. "This is Ozzie. He's looking for a family that doesn't have any other animals. He's good with children, but not with other dogs or cats."

Sam moves to the end of the walk. He kneels and peers in.

"Hi, girl," he says.

I can't see what kind of dog it is, only that Sam seems to be connecting. He's trying to lure the animal over with offers of attention. He sticks a finger inside, but I don't think he's having much luck.

"That's Boo," Dolly says, walking toward Sam. Scarlett and I follow.

"How come she won't come to me?" Sam says.

We peer in the kennel and see a heartbreaking sight. In the far corner sits a dog, facing the wall. Every so often when Sam speaks, the dog leans his head back without turning his body. Just to see who's there.

Dolly puts her hand on Sam's shoulder. "Her owner passed away. She was an older woman who had Boo for three years. I think this baby is just sad. She doesn't understand why she's lost her human. But she's such a sweet girl. We all love her here."

"How long has she been here?" Scarlett asks.

"Too long. I think people misinterpret her sadness for something else."

"What breed is she?" I say.

"She's a mix. I'd say, part beagle, part whippet, who knows what else. But she's a pretty girl."

Sam is in love. I can see it.

"What do you think, Sam?" Dolly says.

"She's the one I want."

He turns and looks up at Scarlett. It's a silent plea that melts our hearts.

"You sure?" Scarlett says.

"Yep. Please. I think she'd be happy with us at the beach. I promise I'll take care of her."

"Are you going to give her a new name?" I ask.

"No," Sam says firmly. "She deserves to keep her name at least. She's lost everything else."

Scarlett takes out her wallet. "Let's make it happen then. We're taking Boo home."

Scene Break

"How's she doing?" I say, looking in the mirror.

"She's fine. She licked my face a minute ago."

Sam's got an arm around the frightened dog. She doesn't know what a lucky day this is for her. She sits perfectly still.

Scarlett's hand reaches back and she wiggles a finger at the dog. "Hello, Boo. I'm so glad we stocked the pantry with food for you."

Sam's face lights up. "Really? Cool!"

. "We have toys and a bed for her. Think we thought of everything," I say.

I make the final turn onto our street and pull into their driveway. Sam's talking to the dog already.

"We're home, girl! Boo, this is our house. Come on, I'll show you around. And we've got the beach, too!"

He gets the dog out of the car and after a vigorous shake it follows his new human.

I look at the grinning girl next to me in the front seat. "You happy?"

"Ecstatic. The entire trip was so perfect. Well, all except your umm, time spent attending to your business."

She tries to say it with a straight face, but it doesn't hold.

"Promise me you'll never refer to that again. I'm trying to forget the whole thing."

"Whatever you need to tell yourself," she says giggling.

Oh God. I can't think about what she most likely smelled and heard.

"In a sharp pivot, let's talk about the fact that I haven't seen you naked in three days. Have I ruined the mood for life?"

She leans across the center divide and puts her nose on mine. "You're not getting rid of me that easily."

"Now that Sam's seen us sleeping in one bed do you think we can occasionally sleep together? Like tonight?"

It takes a few beats for her to answer. I'm crossing my fingers and toes.

"What do you think? I want to say yes. But then we're gonna get used to it, and how could we ever be apart again? Then what?"

"Then we stay together," I say, surer than ever.

"No. You can't make that statement now. Not without knowing there isn't a chance next year or the year after you won't change your mind."

"Yes, I can."

She lowers her eyes and the corners of those luscious lips turn up.

"Sam has to come first in this situation. I've got to protect him, even if it works against me. Let's leave things as they are for now."

I'm certain I look as deflated as I feel, but my head nods while my heart disagrees.

"Okay. But we should take a walk on the beach with Sam and the dog. I need to still the raging hard on I'm about to get thinking about you."

Her delicate hand wraps around my neck.

"Kiss me, you magnificent man."

"Oh that's going to help," I tease.

But I can't refuse her request. Our lips touch and she takes the kiss I give. It's always on another level from kisses I've had before. Something in the way she puts her whole self into the connection. I want to go on kissing her forever.

"Come on, guys!" Sam hollers. "Oh, geez. Whatever."

We part.

"That kid will be the death of me," Scarlett says chuckling.

But I know better. She's taking to her new role, and it only impresses me more.

Scene Change

Boo's timid at first. But the power of the ocean to impress beats her hesitation. It energizes every living creature that sees it. The salty spray, the crashing waves, and the movement of the tide rushing in and pulling back. It wins the dog over.

"I'd say Boo's never been on the sand before," Scarlett says.

I pick up a stick of driftwood and offer it to Sam. "Here, see if she'll fetch. Don't throw it too far into the waves."

He takes it and shows his tail wagging friend who comes close for a sniff.

"Go get it, girl!"

With one throw the dog takes off, eager to do what's been

asked. She wants to play. Not sure this sort of play was ever offered. An old woman wouldn't have had the strength for it.

"That's a good sign," I say. "Think Sam's chosen well."

"Our family just grew. I like this new addition. Look at Sam's face."

But my concentration is on something else. Up ahead three figures are walking toward us. I think it's the boys Sam was with smoking weed.

"There's those boys," I say to Scarlett.

When she looks her face goes serious. But I don't have time to comment because Boo takes off with the sight of approaching people. Obviously losing her former shyness. Maybe all along she was a friendly dog.

Sam starts after her with the leash.

"Boo! Here, girl!"

When he sees who the animal is running for he stops and looks at us.

"I'm coming," I say, going into a jog.

The two of us head for the boys. The dog's going to reach them first. I see one kid pick up a stick in anticipation. When Boo reaches the boys, she jumps on their legs and dances circles around them. Then the boy throws the stick hard into the crashing wave. Fucker.

Boo runs straight into the rolling foamy water but misjudges the strength. The stick's lost, Boo's tumbling and not able to right herself. That's when we get there.

"You fuckers!" Sam yells.

"Stay here," I order Sam.

Then I go in for the dog. The shock of the Atlantic almost steals my breath. And I'm only up to my calves. I spot Boo struggling to keep her head above water and I grab her coat with both hands. There's a look of shock and fear on her face, mixed with gratitude for being rescued.

As I head for the shore I see Scarlett running to meet us. The boys are just standing there looking slightly amused. Assholes.

"What the fuck were you thinking?" I say to the one who threw the stick. The one whose smirk I'd like to punch.

The smallest of the three speaks up. "We were just messin around."

The asshole gives him a death stare.

"Let's go," he commands his minions.

As they walk away, I give one parting shot. "Next time I see you here I'm calling the police. This is a private beach."

A middle finger rises in defiance.

"Fuck you!" Sam calls after them.

My hand wraps around his arm, holding him back from any further comment.

Sam knows better than to contradict or question me. I've got that look that my father used to get when he meant business. It dawns on me. I'm Sam's champion. I haven't been anyone's champion for a long time.

I hand Boo over to him.

"Although I applaud your proper use of the word, let's not start using that. Okay?" Scarlett says.

He knows he wasn't going to get away with it. "Okay."

Now on solid ground, Boo shakes out the saltwater.

"Day one of dog ownership. Think it's going pretty smoothly," I joke.

CHAPTER 20

SCARLETT

February came in like a lion, roaring its arrival. Nature's reflecting what's going on with me. An unexpected storm, dunes hammered and reshaped by strong winds. That's the state of my mind. It's all a whirl.

Then the big warm-up to sixty degrees the weatherman promised didn't pan out. Who cares? There's plenty of heat wherever I go. I've got my love to keep me warm.

Just thinking of the word makes my butt cheeks clench. Because I don't know what to do with the information. I love Parish. How do I know it? Turns out what I've heard all my life is true. You just know. Trying to lie about it to myself would be idiotic. But locked inside my mind's the only place I allow it to exist. Outwardly everything looks the same.

I need time to process. First, does he feel it too? Sometimes it seems he's about to say something then backs away. Then there's the biggest issue of all. What about Sam? His well-being and happiness have to be considered in every decision I make.

And even if Parish feels the way I do, does it carry over to Sam? Shit. Nothing in my life moves in a straight line anymore. Same for Sam. We're a complicated package deal.

I have no intention of telling Parish how I feel. I'm not about to say it first. *Oh no. Not going to happen.*

I'm old fashioned that way. I want him to be the one compelled to declare his love. I don't want to hear the words as just a response to what I've said.

It's become a job keeping it under wraps. Some little monster in my brain is pushing the three words forward. They want out. I'm afraid I'm going to blurt it. Every day I rebury them.

Snapping out of my fantasies, I try to concentrate on more-immediate issues. I've got to make those cupcakes for Sam's class. There's clothes to wash. I should be planning tonight's dinner. But looking out the slider seems infinitely more interesting.

Watching the seagulls picking at the sand, I'm aware how my take on things has changed. Last year I would have laughed if someone had said how attached I'd become to this beach. It's become a pocket of paradise.

It's not just Parish. I've come to love the smell of salty spray, the look of grey angry clouds and the feel of sand between my toes. And the sound of the breathtaking sea. I'm hooked.

Coming around the farthest dune, Parish and Sam move toward the houses. I recognize the cool down. It's a slow unwinding of the jog. Almost walking but not quite. I grab the binoculars.

There's no talking. Each of them look ahead, intent on completing their run, I guess. Then they break off. Parish heads for his steps and Sam angles toward the house.

I return the glasses to their rightful place and take out the cake mix from the pantry. Sam's hard steps can be heard from here. The slider's pushed open.

"I'm back!"

I peek out from the kitchen. "Did you have a good run?"

"Yeah. What's for lunch?"

No matter how many times I've said it, he keeps asking. "Whatever you make yourself," I say.

This time he doesn't laugh. He leans his head back as if what I've said is just too much to take. Now I chuckle.

"I'm sorry you have to actually assemble a sandwich. I realize it's asking a lot."

Now I get a half smile.

"Can't we go to the diner?" he says.

"Sure. Should we ask Parish to join us?"

He lifts his sweatshirt over his head and trades it for the clean one on the hook.

"I don't think that would be a good idea," he says, putting it on.

"Why not?"

"He's sad today."

I put on my jacket and grab the keys. "He is? About Justin?"

"Yeah. It's the anniversary of the shooting."

"Shit. Let me call him before we go. Just to let him know I'm thinking about him."

Sam's hand stops me. He shakes his head.

"He doesn't want to talk."

There's a long pause while I sift through all the information I was just handed. My conclusion is Sam knows what he's talking about. I'll take his advice.

Scene Break

L UIE'S DINER looks the same every time I've been here. Sam and I have become regulars and certain extras come with that. A nod from Oscar the cook, owner and chief bottle washer. A sit down visit from the waitress. If she thinks it, she says it. I like that about her because it's usually funny.

"Here you go," she says, setting down our plates.

She slides in next to Sam and nudges him over with her body. He hardly notices, just edges over and goes for his cheeseburger.

"Where's Parish, honey?" she says. "Writing?"

"Yeah. Sam and I are going to bring him a piece of your lemon meringue."

"His favorite. I'll wrap it up."

Her eyes dart to the door and the unfamiliar two couples that just walked in.

"Freakin' tourists," she says, getting out of the booth.

Sam chuckles his take on the scene and dips a French fry in the catsup.

I get into my BLT and potato salad.

"So, you and Parish didn't talk much today, huh?" As the words leave my mouth I'm conscious of how artless my digging is. He hears it too. I'm not fooling anybody.

"He was talking to the waves," he says as if it's perfectly normal.

He sees the question in my eyes.

"That's when you don't want to talk to another person. You tell the waves. I know. It sounds stupid."

"No, it doesn't. I wish I would have known about this. I've got all kinds of things to tell the waves."

"Sometimes it makes me feel better. Parish does it more than me."

I wipe the corners of my mouth and take a sip of the chocolate shake.

"I hope it helped him today. It was pretty bad, huh?"

"I think I made him sadder," he says, meeting my gaze.

"How?"

"I asked him if his kid knew about talking to the waves."

"I don't think it's out of line. You were just two friends talking."

He shrugs his shoulders and loads more catsup on his plate.

"So what did he say?"

"He said nothing had ever happened to make his son sad. He never needed to talk to the waves."

"Shit."

"How come he never sleeps at our house? With you."

Where the hell did that come from?

"Uh, well, why would he?"

He dips his chin and looks up at me. "I'm not twelve, you know."

That makes me laugh. Out of the mouths of fourteen-year-olds.

"I think he needs to be with us tonight. I mean you. He needs you tonight," he says.

It's at that exact moment I see the good man he could become.

Scene Break

On the way back home, Sam's lost in his phone, texting friends. There's no conversation between us, but I'm not upset. I have Parish on my mind. Do I ask him to spend the night? There's nothing I can come up with to talk me out of the idea.

Am I harming Sam by sleeping openly with Parish at our house? In the back of my mind a crowd of imaginary mothers scream YES! I'm not sure though. I'm pretty sure it's just how I think I SHOULD be thinking. Obviously he knows we're having sex. Otherwise he wouldn't have suggested what he did. I'll pass it by Parish and see what he says.

I pull in to the driveway and turn off the car.

"I'll be back in a few. I'm going to see Parish. Call your grandparents while I'm gone. And ask them exactly when they'll be arriving on Saturday."

There were four comments he could have responded to just now, but instead he's smiling at his phone. My best guess is he's texting Amy. That's the extent of their relationship. I think. That could be the most naïve thing I've ever believed.

I take the quickest route to his house. Around our deck, down the steps, across the sand. When I come around the side of his place, he's on the deck. Sitting in the chair, head back eyes closed.

"Would you like some company?"

His eyes open slowly. They're red. He purses his lips together holding back the sadness.

LESLIE PIKE

"Sam came up with an excellent idea. I want your take on it."

"What's that?"

I climb the stairs and come behind where he sits. Placing my fingertips on his temples, I start to gently rub.

"He asked me why you don't spend the night."

That gets his attention. He turns to face me, with an amused expression.

"You're kidding, right?"

"No. I couldn't come up with an argument. The jig is up, you know."

"I'm good with it. I know you had some hesitations. What are they?"

I quickly try to gather my thoughts, the right words. Oh, fuck it.

"I wanted to be sure we were exclusive. It would send the wrong message to a young boy if we weren't. I have to think like that now."

He gets this adorable look on his face. Kind of like he's shocked I'd think otherwise.

"Scarlett, you must be kidding. We're together all day every day. You're the only woman I want."

"It's settled then," I say, smiling like a goon.

He gets up and takes me in his embrace. My hand traces the shape of his face.

"Thank you."

"For what?" I say.

"For everything."

We seal our words with a long, lovely kiss.

"You know, Valentine's Day is coming," he says.

"I do know that. Will you be mine?"

"I'm that already."

My heart's soaring.

"I have a special present for you. We're going on a little trip. Three days," he says.

"Really? I'm so excited! Where?"

"It's a surprise. I'll give you all the details you need to know tonight when I come over."

Sometimes the world is such a beautiful place.

CHAPTER 21

PARISH

"*I*'m excited and I don't even know what's happening," Scarlett sighs into the phone.

"I'll be there in two minutes. I'm just locking up."

"Are you going to tell me where we're going? Sam and his grandparents should know in case they need to contact us."

"They should. Sam's known for two weeks."

There's a pause followed by a laugh. "You're kidding, right?"

"No. And don't think you're going to get it out of him, or his grandparents. They're in on it too."

"What?"

"I talked with them last night. Let's not waste more time. I'm coming over."

I disconnect, chuckling to myself. Bet she's already headed to Sam's room to interrogate him.

I lift the suitcase into the trunk and slide into the front seat.

My anticipation of the next three days and nights is running high. It took me a week to come up with how we'd celebrate Valentine's Day. I've never wanted to please a woman so much. If someone had told me I'd be doing that, I'd have laughed in their face.

I'm pretty sure what I came up with is perfect. Hope she agrees.

Desire's a stunning sensation. I see now that I had always sold it short. When it went beyond the physical with Scarlett the meaning of the word grew. In its depth. Wanting her physically came easy but craving the emotional connection has been a surprise. I never felt this way before. Not with anyone.

Backing out of the driveway I head for hers.

It's our first weekend away together, our first hotel stay alone. She needs to see how close we are to a different world. Martin's Beach has become a magical spot for me since she arrived. I see it differently than I did before.

It's as if a curtain has lifted. But I'm not sure she sees it the way Sam and I do. The pull to return to Montana might be too strong. I need to convince her this is our place.

There she is, standing in the driveway next to a suitcase and carryon. A little dance breaks out, bringing a smile to my face. Beautiful girl.

I turn in the driveway and pop the trunk.

"Good morning," I say, getting out. "Did you give Sam the third degree?"

"No, dammit. They left a half hour ago for breakfast."

She jumps in my arms and tightly wraps her legs around me.

"Where are we going? I'm not letting go until you tell me."

"That works for me," I say, leaning her against the side of the car. "See. We can be very happy like this."

I pump my dick against her to prove my point. She punches my arm.

"Come on! Tell me."

"First tell me if you packed everything on the list I gave you."

"Yes! I brought it all. The walking shoes, the bathing suit, a sexy dress or two. Sexy lingerie. And your favorite. The red sweater."

"Good. I guess I can let you in on the surprise. We're going to New York. I hope you're still excited."

Her face transforms, eyes widening and mouth curving into a smile.

"God, I love you!" she blurts.

The shock of the moment renders us both silent. Her jaw drops and her eyes widen in horror. She speaks before I can respond.

"I mean, I love that you planned such a great trip for us. It's so cool. New York! What an awesome choice, how did you pick which place?"

"Scarlett," I interrupt her panicked soliloquy. "It's alright. I know what you meant. Don't worry. Sometimes it's just a comment."

We're still against the car, her legs wrapped around me. As if her words have fused us together. But neither makes a move to untangle. She's regretting the statement, I'm wishing it were true. And what's that look she's giving me? I'd swear she wants to say more.

Scene Break

Our hour and twenty-minute flight from Maine to New York turned out to be different than I had imagined. Scarlett did a lot of talking, more than I'd ever heard her do. She didn't leave spaces for lulls in the conversation. Which worked for me, because to tell the truth I wasn't entirely listening.

I was lost inside my head, trying to figure out if what was said was a slip of the tongue. Or as hoped, the truth. *Love?* She denied it.

But something strange is happening. The more she talks about nothing, the more she deflects, the clearer the real message. I think she was right the first time. There's a look in people's eyes when they're in love. I see it in the mirror.

"Oh, Parish this place is gorgeous," Scarlett says as we walk to the hotel elevators.

"I did my research. The Mandarin fits our particular interests," I say with a lifted eyebrow.

She bites her bottom lip and holds back a smile.

"Which interests?"

The elevator doors open and our good luck begins. It's empty. I follow her inside and wait silently for the doors to slide shut.

"Push forty-five," I say.

She does as requested. Her eyes lock on mine and lips part just a bit in anticipation of what's coming. I close the space between us.

Our lips are touching when I say, "We like making love."

I purposely use the word. Repeat it intentionally. It doesn't escape her notice and it doesn't scare her away. Instead her hands reach for my face. A kiss. What an inadequate word for what passes between us. It's otherworldly. Proof of what's happening. And while it's sexy and arousing, it goes beyond that description.

It makes me want to say the thing that hangs unsaid. Risk humiliation. I want to whisper it or scream it. I just need to say the words. Find her eyes and say the thing that scares us both.

But we've reached our destination. The doors quietly slide open. It takes a few beats before our bodies move.

"Let's go see our temple," I say, taking her hand.

She's holding on tightly. Her other hand resting on my arm as we walk to suite seven. I open the door to the impressive space. Our luggage can be seen through the double doors of the bedroom. How'd they do that so quickly? Music plays softly in the background. It's a perfect fit for our tastes. That was one of the questions I was asked when making reservations. There's no detail overlooked.

"Wow! Look at this!" she says.

We're hit by the incredible views. Perched high above Columbus Circle, the living and dining room looks out at quintessential Manhattan. Floor-to-ceiling windows dramatically highlight the bird's-eye view of Central Park and the sea of skyscrapers. A wide curved couch on a thick area rug faces the views.

"Perfect," I say, inspecting the eight hundred square foot space. "This is bigger than my house."

"It's unbelievable."

Sleek and modern is the mood of the Asian-inspired rooms.

"I read the angle of the room is meant to capture the moment at sunset when the city's bathed in tones of amethyst. We'll see if it's true."

There's a look of awe on her face. This is just what I hoped for. I wanted to dazzle the woman.

"You did good," Scarlett says.

"All for you, babe."

She smiles at my name for her.

"Let's look at the bathroom. I want to see where we're going to bathe," she says with a twinkle in her eye.

Walking in, the wall of windows sets the spectacular backdrop. Black marble floors, a huge mirror over black and white marble countered sinks and the shower and tub from a fantasy scene in a movie. They both have rainforest attachments. We're going to use that. I'm already imagining the scene.

"Oh my God! Look at this, Parish. Let's take a bath."

I reach for my zipper. Why waste time?

She stops my hand.

"Let me do that."

She unbuckles the belt and slowly slides it out of its loops. I unbutton the shirt and leave it open for her to play. My nipples harden with the touch of her delicate fingers. Next is the zipper. It's pulled down excruciatingly slow. My dick's talking to her hands, begging for attention.

Before the pants are lowered, her warm hand pulls my briefs away and she slides fingers inside. Instead of a stroke, they wiggle against my skin, right above the base of my dick, then encircle my hardness. Fuck me.

I lift the sweater dress over her head. It comes off in one smooth movement, revealing body beautiful. The bra and panties debut in black lace. Still in red heels, it's about the sexiest vision imaginable.

My eyes travel from her breasts to her eyes. They're inviting me to go further.

I unhook the bra and peel it down, kissing each inch of the reveal. Nipples temporarily stop the slide. I set them free, bra sailing to the floor. God. Taking one then the other in my mouth, we both have an instant reaction. They stiffen against my tongue; my dick hardens against her body.

Lips trail kisses from areolas to stomach. I kneel on the thick rug in front of the tub. She widens her stance.

My mouth acts like a divining rod, finding the buried treasure between her legs. At first, it's on top of the panties. I lick the fabric over her clit. Carefully biting black lace with my teeth, I pull it aside. Fuck. Those lips. Wet already. Tongue finds flesh. I worship her.

Holding my head, she moans the contained sound I love. The music of Drake inspires my rhythm. I'm going to make her come before we even get completely naked.

"Oh, yeah. There. God, Parish."

When I look up her eyes are closed. She's lost in the sensation. I could eat her pussy for the next three days just to keep looking at this expression. With every minute I bring her closer to the edge of the cliff. She doesn't fear the fall. It's the leap that always sets her free.

The moans are less controlled now. She's pushing against my mouth. Fuck me. Fuck me. Fuck me, please.

And then she starts to let it go. I hear the breathing change from labored to freeform breaths of passion.

"Oh, oh, ohhhhhhh," she calls, lost in the feeling.

I grab her round cheeks, half covered in silky lace, pressing her pussy against me. Then I slow my roll, quieting the tongue so not to ruin the sensation with too much pressure.

She falls into the orgasm. It's too strong for words or sounds. Her body stiffens against me. She comes and comes, and I taste the juices that reach my tongue. Oh, woman.

"God. Every time," she says, lifting my chin.

I stand and kiss her. The taste of her perfect pussy on me. She takes her tongue and lightly licks around my lips, getting all of it. A crooked smile paints her face, showing how much she loves the naughtiness.

"Let me start the water," she says, turning on the spigots.

"It fills in less than a minute. That's another reason I picked this place."

By the time we're naked, the water has reached the top of the tub. A twist and tuck of her long hair is expertly done. I help her in.

"When my pussy hits the water, it's gonna boil," she says, taking a careful seat.

Standing in the water, straddling her legs I lean forward balancing myself on the wide surround of the tub. Now my dick's where I want it. She parts her lips and looks up at me.

"Let me love you," she says.

Ohhhhh. She's doing exactly what I did. Dancing around the word. Using it in every other context. Testing the waters.

I smile my impression. "It's all I want."

Before she takes me in her mouth, she places a tender kiss on the tip.

Soft Break

An hour and a half, a mind-altering blow job and a slippery fuck later, we're stepping out of the lukewarm water.

"I want to dry you," I say, grabbing the thick white bath towel from the edge of the tub.

She turns her back to me and untwists her hair. It falls loose in one seductive motion. Coming up behind her I begin to dry.

The skin looks flawless and the shape of her at this angle stunning.

"As a man, let me say this is very sensual," I say, admiring the view.

She looks over a shoulder. "Let's spend the rest of the day and night in bed. Is that alright with you?"

The towel's dropped where we stand, and I don't bother to dry myself off. My answer to Scarlett's question is to pick her naked body up and put her over my shoulder.

"Eeeeep!" she screams.

"To the bed, woman," I say, slapping the velvety, round ass.

The feeling of breasts against my back is my new favorite sensation.

When we reach the huge bed I toss her right in the middle of the down cover. She sinks in the luxurious bedding. Then I pound my chest like a gorilla that just smelled the female in heat. It's unlike me. But she brings out the play.

She throws back the covers, climbs in and locks eyes with me. Sometimes eye contact is more intimate than words will ever be.

"Come here. Take everything I have," she whispers.

It's soft, genuine. I stop with the monkey business and get in bed. Rolling over and leaning on an elbow, I watch her. The light through the windows has changed. It's sunset.

"Look, they weren't kidding. The city looks like a jewel," she says, looking past my shoulder.

I don't turn to see the sunset's show. Everything I'm interested in looking at is right in front of me. The corners of her mouth lift and fingers move a piece of hair from my forehead.

Inside my head a voice is telling me to say it. Tell her. Scream it or whisper, just say it. Find her eyes and say it now.

"I love you, Scarlett."

The words float in the air and settle in her eyes. I'm praying they reach the heart.

Hands reach for my face. "I love you too, Parish. All the way."

We bask in the moment, neither wanting to break this spell.

"Are you certain? You denied it this morning," I tease.

"I thought I scared you. I had to take it back."

"Scared me? Don't you know what you've done for me?"

"I hope I've made you happy."

"You've done more. You brought me back from a dark place. You've made the worst parts of my life bearable. That's not a small thing."

"From now on we'll have each other to share whatever makes us sad. I promise to be your comfort. Will you be mine? You are my Valentine."

"Kiss me, love," I say, not wanting to wait another moment.

"Get in here, baby," she says, arms open wide.

One of Scarlett's gifts is she fills me with feelings I didn't know were there. They show up unannounced. The little moments aren't so little. I know the best part of my day is going to be with her. The way I know she's the one. The only one for me.

Love is real. I'm glad I waited for it.

CHAPTER 22

SCARLETT

*O*nly narrow trails of chocolate remain on the bowl lined in real edible gold. There isn't a trace of white coffee ice cream left. Le Coucou has lived up to its reputation as one of New York's finest French restaurants.

The double row of chandeliers and the soft French love songs set the romantic mood of the room.

"Thank you for giving me the last bite," I say, raising the champagne glass.

"You're welcome. Have you had a good night?"

"I'll never forget it, Parish. Had I told you I always wanted to see the Phantom?"

"You mentioned it."

"See, that's one of your strengths. You pay attention."

I pour the last of the champagne, splitting it between us. It's the first alcohol I've had.

"I've got a question," I say.

"Ask me."

"It's about Sam. I've been thinking about how us being in love affects him."

He takes a big breath and fidgets in his chair.

"Does that make you nervous?" I say chuckling.

"Not at all. I'm just trying to think of how to say what I mean."

"Well, he and I are together for life now. If you and I are together does it mean you love him too? Is that what we aim for?"

His expression softens. "Scarlett, I've aimed successfully for friendship with Sam. I think that's the right thing to do. His father just died. Do you think he's going to love another man in that way so soon? Or for that matter, I love another child? It doesn't work that quickly."

I roll his words around my mind.

"That's not to say it can't grow to love," he continues. "But first he and I need to build respect and affection. I'm pretty happy with how close we are already. We genuinely like each other."

"That sounds right. I'm just so out of my depth with this mother-figure role. And now there's a new unfamiliarity. I'm in love. So be patient with me."

"I think Sam and I have a better chance at getting to love if we walk slowly toward it."

Sometimes the fact Parish is a writer bubbles up. He's so good at expressing himself.

"And let's vow to do this. Talk everything out. Okay?" I say.

He reaches for my hand across the table. Our fingers entwine.

"Yes. I want that too. And just know I'm mindful of Sam's vulnerability. I'm going to be what fathers are. A male voice, a protector and someone who has his interests in mind. Shall we start there?"

I let his words settle in my heart. I think this is going to work beautifully.

Scene Break

Memories of the past week float freely. I'm pretty sure I've rinsed this plate twice. My one-track mind can only concentrate on Parish. It wants to stay close to him, live in the image of his face, go over his body in detail.

Then to make it absolutely perfect I replay the moment he first said he loved me.

What an incredible feeling that was. Love flowed between us, his to me and mine to him. I didn't think our lovemaking could get any better. I was wrong about that. There's a new kind of tenderness that love has brought, mixed with the passion we've felt from the start.

And the most stunning realization is that I have both feet on the ground. This isn't a romance based on unicorns and butterflies. Its root is in the real. We started in the storms of life. Our love was forged in them.

I'm choosing not to think too far ahead. We need to live in our love for enough time to know its strength. To figure out its direction. I've known where my heart's going, I've already dipped a toe in the idea. But I could be alone in that leap. Only time will prove it all.

Sam should be home from school soon. Boo's taken her post. It's getting to be that time of the day, and she stands guard by the back door. They've become a team, she and Sam. That bond formed on the first day. They've become each other's protector.

I watch Parish coming up the stairs with the Monopoly game he retrieved from his house. That red hoodie looks hot on him. But then everything does.

Every day since we got back from New York he's been slowly moving an item or two from his house to ours. He's not fooling anyone. Sam thinks it's funny. Last night when he suggested Parish hire the local moving company, it made us all laugh.

"Where do you want this?" Parish says, coming through the slider.

"Leave it on the dining table. We can play tonight."

"I just got off the phone with my sister. Her husband's going on a business trip in a couple of weeks. She's going to stay at my place."

I give him a meaningful stare. "And you? Where are you staying?"

He picks up an apple and takes a bite. "Here, of course."

"Parish, you see your sister once every five years. Don't you think you should stay there with her?"

"No."

My head tilts a doubting stare.

"What?" he says, knowing full well what I'm saying.

I just chuckle.

"There's no reason to have to sleep in the same house," he says. "I'll spend all day and evening with her. But when it's lights out I'm heading to Casa Scarlett."

Wrapping my arms around his neck, I kiss his nose.

"You're a horny son of a bitch."

"My being horny has nothing to do with it. Well, maybe ten, twenty percent. I just like being with you."

I can't fight that. I feel the same.

The sound of the dog's bark pulls our attention.

"I'm home!" Sam calls from the hall. "Stop kissing."

I untangle my arms from Parish's neck and turn to greet our returning scholar.

"See, I knew you two would be doing that," he says, entering the room.

"We're not doing anything!" I say laughing.

"Yes we were," Parish teases. "You just ruined a beautiful moment."

That's the great thing about their relationship. Already they've built this rhythm to their conversations. Both know exactly when they're teasing and when it's serious. I like watching the friendship build. What Parish said the other night really set things straight for me.

Sam wouldn't respond to a pushy guy. Never. He'd back off. Parish saw that before I figured it out. Now the foundation is being laid. I'm happy. So happy.

"Up for a walk? Or a run?"

The dog hears her second favorite trigger word. It comes right after treats. Ears perk up and tail wags a response. Take me! Take me too!

Sam drops his backpack on the counter and grabs the leash.

"Yeah, let's go."

The sound of Parish's cell interrupts their march to the slider. Sam's face shows his impatience. The dog's not too happy about the delay either. When he looks at who's calling, he waves them forward.

"I gotta get this. It's my publisher. Go ahead. I'll catch up in a few minutes."

Dog and boy don't hesitate. They're out the slider, down the stairs and on the sand before Parish takes a seat on the couch.

It's a joy watching them in the bright sun of this February afternoon. The ocean is churning. The dog is energized and running at full speed. They've got the entire beach to themselves.

This is what youth looks like. A boy and his dog. Hopefully Sam's not thinking of things that could make him sad. Every day I look for that expression he wears when he's thinking of his parents. Today it wasn't there. I'll take it. Even if it's just for a day. Blessed peace.

"Alright. I'll be sending it by Monday or Tuesday at the latest," Parish says. "Talk to you at the end of the week."

He disconnects.

"This is the first time I've missed my deadline. It's all your fault," he says, getting up.

"My fault?"

Taking me in his arms, he shares his theory. "I'm pretty sure it's because so much of my writing time has been usurped by how much time is required to satisfy you. You want to fuck all the time. It's exhausting."

There's a beat before we both start laughing at the absurdity and partial truth of the statement.

"Well, there's an easy fix. Let's make a schedule. Say, twice a week, for a half hour at a time. That should leave you plenty time to write."

He gets a horrified look on his face.

"Stop! No! I'd rather write less and be in bed with you more."

"Then quit your complaining," I say, slapping his firm ass.

I see his eyes dart to the slider behind me. And an expression comes over his face I've never seen before. When I turn I see why.

"God dammit," he says softly.

Out on the sand, close to the shore, a blonde curly headed child kneels. The lighthouse keeper and a younger woman stand watching the sandcastle being built. All three are bundled against the cold.

I press Parish against me and lay my head on his chest.

But it's no comfort. He untangles my arms from around his back and steps away. Walking to the slider he grabs the binoculars Sam left on the end table.

He's focused on the child. I know there's nothing he wants to hear. So I just lay my hand on his back in a wordless acknowledgment of his pain.

When he lowers the glasses and turns to me he's about to cry. Silently and without a change in expression. Closed eyes and a shake of his head speak the depth of his agony.

"I'm going back to my place for a little while. Don't worry."

He kisses the top of my head, sets the binoculars on the table and walks out. My heart's pounding. I'm not sure if I should follow him or let him do what he chooses. Shit!

I watch him take the stairs and cross the sand. He hasn't looked away from the group at the shoreline. Then I lose sight of him when he goes around the corner of his house.

Tears well in my eyes and the lump in my throat starts to ache. What do I do? It only takes me a few seconds to come to the only conclusion that makes sense. Give him his alone time. He needs to process. I only hope he's changed his methods of coping.

Of course he has. I haven't seen him in that dark place for months. He's completely reined in the out-of-control drinking. That was all before we met. He never slept on the beach after that first night.

Relax, Scarlett.

This is how grief plays out. I'm beginning to understand. My grief for Kristen, and even Sam's for his mother, doesn't look the same as Parish's for his son. His is a wound that will never completely close no matter what it looks like on the surface. Underneath the scar it's raw.

What's this? He's leaving the house, hood up and dark glasses on. Oh no, is he walking toward the child? Is that a good idea, or the worst one he's ever had? I grab the binoculars.

About halfway to the water he makes a sharp right and avoids our neighbor and his guests. Good. That makes sense. I can't see any good outcome if they spoke.

He's probably trying to catch up with Sam. Somehow he knows how to handle Parish's moods with the least amount of conversation. Just two guys not talking it out.

There's a long list of things I wanted to get to today, but no chance I'll get to any of them. I'll be sitting on the deck pretending to read my romance novel until I see them returning.

Soft Break

The sky's getting dark and for the last half hour the waves have been steadily building. The lighthouse keeper and his family are starting back. Where are the boys? I had to retreat to the house ten minutes ago when it just got too damn chilly. Then I hear the barking.

Damn, I left the binoculars outside on the table.

Opening the slider and stepping into the cold, I grab the glasses. Lifting them to my eyes I try to spot Parish and Sam. The wind's whistling and salty mist settles on my face.

Where are they? Then I see the dog. She's running full force along the shoreline, focused on the stick Sam just threw. The dog retrieves it, pivots and runs back with it between his teeth. She offers it to Sam. I move the binoculars to the right, looking for Parish.

He's coming around the dunes. Why's he so far behind? What's that in his hand? Shit! It's a bottle. The same size and brand he was drinking the night I covered him with Sam's blanket. As far as I can see it's empty. I wasn't expecting this. He trips and almost goes down.

Then the unexpected happens. In an instant his face transforms from a detached expression to the most focused stare I've ever seen. He takes off running full force, dropping the bottle and throwing his sunglasses off to the wind. I swing the binoculars to the left and see the horrifying sight. Sam's being tossed in the crashing sea. The dog's in the curl of a wave, one leg sticking out in a disgusting sight. Unnatural.

I'm off.

Down the steps.

Onto the sand.

Running and screaming against the wind. Calling Sam's name. By now I can see Parish in the water, frantically searching for Sam. His back's to a huge wave that beats him to the sand. Oh God! Help us! Help Sam! Please! I feel like I'm in a dream, moving in excruciatingly slow motion.

CHAPTER 23

PARISH

*T*hese are deadly waters. All the energy of the waves in the shallows. I expect some loss of control, but instead I'm tossed around like a rag doll, about to take a certain beating.

Don't panic!

I'm slammed into the concrete sand by the one I didn't see coming. My head taking the blow.

Where's Sam? Where is he?

The water's murky, freezing, churned by the relentless sea. I rise and try to suck a breath of air. This is the sloppy water surfers talk about. Waves of different sizes coming from different directions. It makes the air hard to find when you finally come up for a breath. The sight and sounds of the ocean are humbling. Hard to face.

Scarlett. She's trying to come in. There's no time to stop her.

Sam's in more danger.

God, help us all! I beg you!

It's tall chop. I swallow a mouthful of saltwater. Don't panic! I spit the water out and take as deep a breath as I can.

Swim to the bottom. The energy of the waves is weaker there.

Maybe I'll be able to see further. My eyes search the water for a sign of Sam. His white sweatshirt or something.

Far off, above my head I see the dog's legs moving furiously, uncontrollably, in the light of a foamy crest.

Can't save her. It would take my focus off finding Sam.

It's getting hard not to be disoriented. My head. Something's happening. Not one hundred percent sure which way is up. When I find him, I'll aim for that light that pierces the foam. That's up. That's where I'll surface.

Where is he? Where is he, God!

In my mind my father's voice speaks. *How long can you hold your breath for? Every breaking wave lasts ten seconds. There's another ten between them. If you can hold your breath for a minute you can survive three sets. But you have to be calm.*

I need air, Dad. Then I'll try.

I do what I know. I exhale underwater, as much as possible. Letting go the air in my lungs. That should help me take a breath more quickly.

I surface.

Waves, wind, spray. There's less of a window in which to pull air. Miraculously I get a good one.

I dive under the waves, head pounding relentlessly.

Stay conscious!

My eyesight is getting foggy. They're burning. The field of vision narrows.

A sense of unspeakable dread washes over me.

Am I going to lose another child?

Am I crying underwater? Is it even possible?

Then I see it.

Sam's lifeless body.

It floats free of any muscle contraction or struggle. Tossed by the violent sea.

He's turned over by the roll of the waves. I see his face. Mouth open. Eyes staring.

In a move I can't really explain, I propel my body toward him with a force I've never known.

This is it. The one shot I'll get.

If it isn't already too late.

My fingers lock onto his wrist and then his sweatshirt with such force it's like a vice.

The one thing working in my favor is we're close to shore.

Just need to get him in.

I pull and push, making slow headway against the raging walls of water.

Work with me, God.

As we head forward I see Scarlett and the lighthouse keeper. He's holding her back until we get close enough for them to help.

Then he releases her and they both rush in.

Careful! It can suck you out before you realize!

The man's stronger. At least he's felt the pull of the water when he casts a line. Scarlett's out of her depth.

Her face is contorted in horror, mouth open in what looks like a scream. But I can't hear anything other than the waves, rising and slamming with such force they actually make the ground shake.

I'm on solid ground!

I stand on jellied legs carrying Sam safely away from the water and laying his body on firm sand.

For a moment I consider not turning his neck, but the risk doesn't outweigh what I know to be true. He drowned.

Clear the mouth of water.

I turn his lifeless body to the side and watch the water pour out.

"Call an ambulance!" I scream with graveled vocal cords.

Sounds of Scarlett and the lighthouse keeper's voices are beginning to get louder but I can't make out the words yet. But they're nodding and pointing at something.

Putting an ear to Sam's mouth, I wait.

No breath.

I cup my hands around the space to block out the wind.

I feel no rush of air.

I lift his limp hand and check for a pulse.

Nothing.

"Sam! Breathe, breathe!" I hear Scarlett's heartbreaking plea as it rises over it all.

"The ambulance is on its way! Hold on, boy!" the lighthouse keeper cries.

He takes Sam's hand and tries to warm the skin with his.

I begin CPR, learned years ago when Justin started swimming.

My thoughts come quickly now, half thoughts, tangents.

Someone can survive if you get to them soon, and if the water's cold enough. Especially children. Someone said that.

I can't remember if I do compressions first or breaths.

I choose breaths. Coupling my lips around the gaping mouth. His lips are blue.

Five full breaths from my mouth to his. Oh no. I'm getting dizzy. Fuck you, God! Fuck you, you merciless piece of shit. I'm not going to pass out!

Then I start the compressions. How many do I do? I think it was more than I had thought.

A number pops into my consciousness. One hundred and twenty.

The count starts.

With one palm placed over the other I push. One, two, three.

"Save him, Parish! Please, save my boy," Scarlett pleads.

"Sshtnd wazs," I say, unable to form words properly.

"What's wrong with him," the lighthouse keeper says.

"He's drunk!"

She's covering her face, crying.

I'm drunk? No.

I have to do one thing. Help Sam. Keep counting.

The lighthouse keeper takes Scarlett in an embrace, but she pushes him away.

"Thirty-five, thirty-six, thirty-seven."

There's no reaction coming from Sam. Just the movement of his cold body in response to violent compressions.

Scarlett begins to wail. I recognize the sound. It's made of horror and earthshaking reality. Where have I heard it before? Now I remember. Me. Justin.

Tears are streaming down my face. I can't see a thing clearly. And it's more than the fact I'm crying. I'm pretty sure there's something wrong with my head, my thinking. Did I get hit by something? How did it happen?

I keep going. And going. My arms are aching with the Herculean effort.

Scarlett falls to her knees. The lighthouse keeper begins to pace.

The wail of an ambulance gets louder and louder. Come save Sam Boy.

One hundred and seventeen, a hundred and eighteen…

Suddenly Sam's body vomits seawater and he sucks in his first breath.

My body lets go of every last thing it has to give.

Scene Break

"Mr. Adams, Mr. Adams wake up."

Like coming down a foggy patch of road into the light, I open my eyes.

"There you are. Parish, I'm nurse Regina. You're in O'Conner Hospital. You've suffered a concussion. You took quite a beating in those waves."

My throat is so sore. I lift my hand to it.

"You swallowed a lot of seawater. Let's see if you can answer a few questions. How many fingers am I holding up?" she says.

"Two." My voice is raspy.

"That's right. Can you tell me your name?"

"Parish Adams."

"You're passing with flying colors. Now for a hard one. What month is this?"

"It's the end of February."

She takes an instrument off the tray next to where she stands.

"Let's check your eyes."

I put a hand up. "Wait. How's Sam? The boy they took from the beach. Did he survive?"

When she smiles I know all's right with the world.

"He's going to be fine. Thanks to you, I hear."

"No lasting damage? He'd drowned by the time I found him," I say, tears filling my eyes.

"He was lucky. You got to him within the first five minutes of submersion. You did good."

"What about oxygen deprivation?"

"The cold seawater slowed his heartbeat and redirected blood flow to his heart and brain. It preserved his vital organs."

"Is he here in the hospital? I'd like to go see him."

A funny look comes over her face. Like she has to tell me something I'm not going to like. The slight hesitation in her answer makes me think she's trying to find the right words.

"You need to rest. I'll tell his nurse you asked about visiting."

I throw back the blanket and sheets. "No. I've got to see him. And his mother. I want to speak to her."

Her hand stops my forward movement. She stands in front of me, blocking my exit.

"The mother has a no-visitor request. We have to honor her wishes."

I chuckle at the thought of being barred from Scarlett and Sam's side.

"I'm sure that doesn't apply to me. Move, please."

But she stays put. A firm look on her face.

"I'm afraid it's specifically about you. The mother doesn't want you there."

What's going on? This is a mistake.

"What room are they in?"

"There's no room phones in his unit. Just wait till you're strong enough."

She's interrupted by the man peeking in the room. The lighthouse keeper knocks on the door.

"Up for a visit?"

The nurse is just happy she doesn't have to continue with our conversation. She waves him inside.

"It'll be good for Mr. Adams to have a conversation. But don't stay too long. I'll be back to do your vitals."

As she leaves the room, my visitor trades spots with her. He stands next to where I lay and pats my hand affectionately.

"You did a tremendous job of saving the boy. I just want you to know that."

"Were you there the whole time? I'm foggy on the details."

"I was there," he says, lifting his eyebrows with the memories. "My daughter and grandchild were with me. Do you remember that?"

"I think so. He was building sandcastles."

"That was the first time we saw you. Sam passed us first, then five minutes later you walked by in his direction."

It's coming back.

"About a half hour or so later we were about to start back to the house. But my grandson heard your dog barking. So we sat on the sand watching Sam throw a stick for the dog to retrieve."

The scene gets clearer.

"Wait! What about the dog? Did she make it out?"

His mouth sets hard as he shakes his head.

"Fuck."

The news stuns.

"When you came around the point we spoke briefly. Do you remember that?" he says.

"Yeah. I asked your grandchild how old he was."

LESLIE PIKE

"Right. Then you kept walking. By the time we stood and had walked for a few minutes we saw what was happening. You were already in the water."

It comes back clear. Horribly clear.

"Scarlett was running from the house. My daughter called 911. I sent her back with the child. You know the rest."

"Thank you for everything you did to help," I say, still holding the images.

"I didn't do much. Just tried to stop her from going in after you."

"That was what I couldn't do. It was a lot."

"I just came from Sam's room," he says. "Actually, from outside the room. There's a no-visitors sign. But Scarlett saw me and she came out."

"Do you have any idea why she doesn't want me there?"

"Yep. When I praised your efforts she shut me down. Said you'd been drinking excessively when the accident happened. I don't know, son, I think she's mistaken."

I feel the confusion coming back, but this time it's not concussion related.

"I wasn't drinking at all. I have no idea why she's saying that."

"I told her we had talked just prior to the accident and I hadn't noticed any signs of you being inebriated. No signs whatsoever of you having had liquor."

"Thank you for that. I've got to get her straight on this."

"Good luck. She strikes me as a woman who's hard to reason with when she's made up her mind."

"What about Sam? Hasn't he set her straight?"

"She said he can't remember anything about the afternoon."

CHAPTER 24

SCARLETT

"*Y*ou have thirteen messages," the answering machine announces.

Our landline has never seen so much action. It's all the family members and friends who don't have my new cell number.

Even Parish left messages. Every day until I sent the letter. It's been silence since then. Now there's no going back. It's done. I wish I could get the words out of my head, but they're mine and I can never undo what was written, even though I made sure to acknowledge he saved Sam's life.

Fragments of sentences float in my mind.

I need to think of Sam...your demons are too strong...you were drinking and not watching. We have to leave this place.

The horror is it's all true. I'm not exaggerating. I can't take on one more damaged soul. As it is I'm handling two. Sam and me. It would be cruel to expose him to a man who can't get through the sadness. Then Sam might not either.

This is the hard part. The time between what was and what will be. Life without him. My stomach twists in knots with the thought.

"I want to talk with you," my father says, walking into my bedroom.

He gives a rap on the open door then comes in before I have a chance to respond.

"What is it?"

"You've got a problem on your hands. And you need to fix it."

I'm rethinking asking my parents' help with bringing Sam home from the hospital. After the accident we both needed the support of our family. But we didn't want to have to rehash and explain everything. At least I didn't.

It hasn't helped a bit, because Sam is still so angry. At me. My rule for Sam not to not talk to Parish without me there has gone over like a lead balloon. I'm not ready to see him and may never be. I expect Sam to disobey me at any time.

My father shuts the door. His face wearing a troubled look.

"Sam needs to be given a chance to thank the man who saved him. What's this about, honey?"

"It's about the fact I need to separate him from people who don't have the ability to protect a child properly," I say, folding my laundry.

"Last week you were pretty sure he checked all the boxes. Your mother told me you were in love with him. What changed?"

I sit on the edge of my bed, feeling defeated.

"That day, right before I saw Sam in the water, I saw Parish. He was walking far behind Sam. And he was carrying an empty whiskey bottle."

His eyebrows come together.

"And he was so drunk, he tripped and almost fell."

"Were you aware of his problem before that day?"

"That's the ugly part I didn't want to have to admit. The first time I saw Parish he was passed out on the sand. Sleeping his drunk off."

He looks at me like only a parent can. One look and I know what I did wrong.

"I know, Dad. I chose to believe it was all in the past. I had good reason to think that. And he had suffered so much. But obviously his sorrows are too strong."

He takes a seat next to me and pats my knee.

"I hardly know the man, so I can't contradict anything you say. But I do know my grandson and he's hurting."

"I don't know what to do," I say softly.

"Somehow Parish's friendship has made Sam's sorrow bearable."

I tip my head to the side in wordless acknowledgement of his point.

And in the moment, I realize how Parish did the same for me. My griefs only outlet was with him. I had to soften it in front of Sam.

My father's arm wraps around my shoulders.

"Now our boy needs to have the closure talking with his friend will bring. I could go with him. Why don't you let that happen? Listen to your papa," he says, lifting my chin.

Tears roll down my face and my lip quivers. I nod.

"Okay then. I'll go tell him you said yes."

He leaves before I can change my mind.

I feel stuck to the bed. I want to disappear right where I sit and not have to imagine their conversation. Or his face. It wouldn't be good to picture his mouth or his beautiful eyes. It would do nothing but weaken my resolve.

Because despite it all, I love him. Regardless, here's where I prove I have what it takes to raise a child. You put them first.

Scene Break

The first five minutes were tough. I kept myself busy avoiding the windows, the slider, the binoculars. But this is ridiculous. It's five friggin o'clock. It's been a half hour. Where are they? And now I've taken guard at the slider, binoculars to my eyes.

"What are you hoping to see, Scarlett?"

My mother's putting me through the third degree while she makes her potato soup.

"Why is it taking so long? What are they talking about?"

"If you'd talk with the man you'd know."

Putting the glasses down I join her at the kitchen counter.

"Why would I do that to myself? It's taking everything I have to hold steady."

"I think you're moving too fast," she says.

Aurora never uses more words than necessary. But she gets to the meat of a conversation every time.

"What's slowing things down going to get me, Mom? A more painful breakup? You, of all people, are telling me to disregard my good sense?"

I start chopping the onions. Aggressively. I don't give a damn if I cry more.

She stops me with a hand to my forearm. "What I'm suggesting is you use both your head and heart. Here's the facts. You love each other. He's great with Sam. He's gone through a horrible loss and still knows how to be gentle and genuine."

Her words soak in, pushing my hard heart to the side.

"And, most importantly, Sam told me he never saw him inebriated after he met you."

"But how about what I saw? What about that?"

"Scarlett, believe half of what you see. Then confirm your hypothesis."

The sound of the slider opening pulls my attention. I move to the living room to see Sam wearing an angry expression. My father seems very calm.

"You ruined everything!" Sam says, starting to cry.

He moves by me without another look and heads for his room.

When I look at my father he's holding up a hand telling me not to follow yet. He locks eyes with my mother and with a lift of his chin signals her to go to Sam.

"What happened?" I whisper.

"I'm not entirely sure because I waited on the deck while Sam went inside."

My shoulders slump with the news. I thought I'd at least find out some kernel of information. I don't have to wait long, because I hear Sam's footsteps returning. He enters the room with my mother close behind.

"He's leaving. Are you happy?" he says, wiping tears away.

I put out my arms in a desperate gesture. He stops me.

"Leaving? No, I'm not happy. Not in the least bit. But, Sam, you need to understand it's my job to protect you now."

"From what? He didn't do anything but risk his life to save mine." The last few words disappearing in his sob.

Now he really starts to cry and buries his face in his hands. It's killing me.

"Sam, you may not believe it but Auntie Scarlett is sacrificing to make sure you're well looked after," my father says.

"None of you were in there talking to him. He didn't do anything wrong," he cries.

I take him firmly by the shoulders.

"Okay, I need to talk to you as if you were an adult, Sam. Just so you see where I'm coming from. That day you almost drowned, Parish was drunk. He probably didn't even know how far away he was from you. I saw it. He was carrying an empty bottle of whiskey just like he had the night I found him sleeping on the beach. His problems aren't behind him at all, like I thought. He's still using them as crutches."

He shakes off my grip.

"What? No, he wasn't drunk. I was with him when he picked up that bottle. He always picks up things we might step on and hurt ourselves with. That was one of his old bottles from before he met us. He told me sometimes he still finds them."

Oh shit.

Everyone's staring at me, watching for my reaction. The air

has been sucked out of the room. They'd be surprised to know how quickly I'm weakening, how badly I want to be wrong.

"But when I accused him of being drunk that horrible day he didn't deny it," I add as a final point.

"He had a concussion, Scarlett. One of the symptoms is confusion. Another is amnesia," my mother says.

"You can't expect someone to answer questions or think clearly enough to defend themselves. Not in those circumstances," my father adds.

Sam's eyes lock on mine and a silent message passes from him to me. *Make it right.*

"I'm sorry, Sam. Really sorry. I'm going to try to talk with Parish."

You'd have thought I just presented him with The Golden Ticket. His whole face changes. There's a ray of hope.

He takes me by my forearms and gives me a pointed stare. "He's leaving for the airport early tomorrow morning. Make him stay."

Soft Break

Alright. My one advantage is that I know he's inside the house. Three cell phone calls went ignored. On the last one I left a message.

I was wrong. Let's talk.

I left out the part I'm coming over. Didn't want to give him the chance to escape before I plead my case.

I grab my heaviest jacket, a knit beanie, and the gloves I set on the table by the door.

"Alright, I'm going over there. I don't know when I'll be back. Nobody come get me."

I know my father started to say something, but I don't wait. I'm out the slider and down the steps. Crossing the sand, I take a few deep breaths of the cold February air.

I'm not going to think it out or plan my apology. I'll just let it flow and hope he hears how desperate I am for forgiveness.

Shit. He's shut off the deck lights. Now I can't see through the glass. Not with the early evening light that remains. I climb the steps and stand at his door. I ring the bell.

Every second is torture. After half a minute or so I try again, this time with an added knock.

Nothing.

I go to the slider and press my nose to the glass. I can't see a thing. So I start talking, hoping Parish is listening.

"I'm sorry. I'm so sorry. Can we talk?"

I see nothing, there's not a sound coming from inside.

"I was wrong. What can I do to make things right with you?"

I feel the tears well. I rest my head on my forearm against the glass.

"Please, Parish," my voice softens. "Will you forgive me for doubting you and for being a colossal asshole?"

I give it a minute or so in case my sense of humor reaches him. Nothing. Quiet.

"What you did for Sam was extraordinary. You're the one who acted like a parent would. Me, I let my insecurities about our past take over. I blew it. I brought you and Sam more pain. It kills me knowing that because all I've wanted is make both your lives better."

I'm making myself cry because it all sounds so hopeless.

"Parish. Please talk to me. I love you. Look what we've survived. We can survive this."

I pause for a few beats.

"We can love each other through the darkness. And you can guide me as I trip my way through my new identity."

Still complete silence. I'm not sure he's even listening. But on the off chance he is, I keep talking.

"Please don't go. Because this thing we have, it won't end just because we've said goodbye."

That's it. I could keep telling him I was wrong and how sorry I am. I could tell him I'll never make the same mistake again. But maybe I just need to give him time to absorb what I've said. I position the deck chair close to the slider and sit. Waiting.

And waiting. And waiting some more. Until the last light of day is replaced by the cover of night. As night falls, the lights in the sky multiply. But only the full moon illuminates where I sit uncomfortably biding my time.

I check my cell. Shit. Almost eight. I'm hungry, and double fucking spent. Physically, emotionally, in every way possible. Should I call my dad to bring food and a blanket and pillow? That wouldn't work. I want Parish to know I'm all in. I'm not going to let a grumbling stomach or toe-numbing cold stop me. If I have to I'll spend the night here.

Wait. My body is tingling with the idea that just popped into my head. Boy, you know when something is so right. I need the grand gesture to get his attention. To force him out. This is genius. If I survive.

As I rise I leave one last message aimed toward the slider.

"I know you're in there. And I'm betting on something my mother told me when I was young. She said you never have to chase what wants to stay."

With that I give up an uncomfortable nest for a much worse one. I head for my sandy bed.

As soon as I get to the bottom of the steps I'm hit with the full force of the cold. Yikes! Oh Jesus. I'm going to have to half bury myself in the closest dune. Yeah, it's perfect really. That's the one Parish was next to that first night.

My hands and feet are already cold through gloves and boots. But I keep moving forward.

I'll just pick my spot on the opposite side of the dune. The side facing his house. Being seen is the whole point. I reach the dune. Thank God. Using my thick gloved fingers, I dig out a hollow. As soon as I plop down and angle my body inside the shallow depression, I know I can do this.

I wait and watch. He's going to come out that door any moment now.

Any moment.

Yeah.

Right now.

One, two, three, NOW!

Fuck me.

Maybe he's in the bathroom or taking a shower.

Or maybe it's really over.

The wind's coming up. I pull my cap over my eyes and lean my head back against the dune.

Soft Break

It's cold climbing this mountain. There's my sister. She's already reached the top before me. She's waving. That Sherpa is wrapping her in a warm beach blanket... Scarlett...Scarlett...Scarlett wake up. What?

I begin to come out of the dream. I don't want to leave Kristen.

"Scarlett!"

I wake with a start and pull my beanie away. A blanket has been laid on me from neck to toe.

"One good turn deserves another," he says smiling.

I'm crying with joy.

"I'm so cold," I say, teeth chattering. "And I'm so afraid you don't love me anymore."

He extends his hand helping me upright.

"That's not how it works, crybaby," he says, taking me inside his big jacket and touching his cold nose to mine.

"It's not?"

"No. I don't want to remember you in fragments. You're the only one I ever showed my heart to. And the reason no one will ever see it again. Just have a little more faith in me."

"Promise." I encircle my arms around his waist and hold on tight.

"I'll never be happier than I am right now," I say.

"I think I can prove you wrong."

I look up into his loving eyes and wait.

"Sam called. The dog was found alive two beaches down. It took time to find us because the chip was still registered to the previous owner. We're getting Boo back tomorrow."

He kisses the top of my head and I lean against his chest.

And in this perfect moment I feel my spirit lift. Grief and struggle, want and need, all becoming something new. Everything I hoped for and all I'm meant to be has been here all along. On this grey, cold, beautiful spot on earth. On the beach in winter.

EPILOGUE

SCARLETT

ugust

MAKE SURE TO REMEMBER ME, the ocean calls.

As if I could forget.

It's sunrise. Sam and Parish are walking to the lighthouse one last time, to see the sun's spectacular arrival. When I watched them with the dog, the scene told a story. Boo wants nothing to do with the water. In fact, she always makes sure one of them are between her and the waves.

We're leaving Martin's Beach today. Now that the day's here I only taste bittersweet. I wish we had one more night to fall asleep to the sound of the waves.

Sometimes you just need to do what's best. For Sam, Parish, and even for me. No matter its beauty, this beach will always hold sad memories for each of us. We need no constant reminders of our losses and near losses. They live inside our souls.

We came to the conclusion that staying here on this beach isn't the way forward. There's a new story for us, someplace else. One that isn't heavy with what wounds us. Montana waits. Sam and I already are connected to it. Parish will feel it too. I'm sure of that.

He won't be hiding from anything there. He said wherever we are will be home for him. I picture him writing in his office looking out at the mountains. Wonder if he'll be wearing his uniform of boxer briefs and his comfy sweaters? Hope so. I think he picked the house solely on that room.

But images of he and I and our beginning will live with me forever. The first time I saw his face peeking out the door, butterscotch candies floating in the shallow waters of the shore, his expression seeing me naked for the first time. I could write a book about the way he whispers and laughs and looks. And how he loves me.

He and Sam went for their last run on the beach. But as I watched there wasn't much running involved. They were too busy talking. I'd like to have been a bird flying overhead listening to the conversation. They never run out of things to discuss. Especially now that Sam's maturing by the day.

Halfway to fifteen is a new place. He's getting taller, I swear it changes weekly. He's adorable. And although I might be prejudiced, I suspect he'll be a girl magnet at his new school in September.

My brothers have made our transition smooth by handling the things we couldn't do from afar. They never fail in their love and support. My dear parents are our steady touchstones, always our champions.

My cell sounds. A text from Sam.

Come to the lighthouse! The Keeper is letting us go to the top! Battery low.

Oh, fun! I always wanted to see the view from there.

I slip the cell into the pocket of my white jeans and check my image in the mirror. Parish likes this navy and white striped top. I'm good to go. As I walk out the slider my shoes get kicked off, but I take them with me. We'll be climbing the metal staircase.

What a beautiful day it is already. The sand is warming, and the seagulls are flying. I'm always looking for the one Parish told us about. The one that kept shitting on his face. But I've never seen it. And he hasn't either. Maybe the bird left to find other souls who needed wake up calls.

Up ahead I see Sam and the dog running toward me. It warms my heart to see Boo at full speed. Full of life. We expected some residual effect after having been through what she experienced. But no. You'd never know.

"Auntie!" Sam calls as he reaches me.

"Did you come to escort me?" I tease.

"No! I need to use the bathroom. Bye!"

Poor guy. He runs past me, taking the dog with him.

The lighthouse looks beautiful in the early morning light. Parish stands in front watching and waiting for me. He holds up something and shakes it. Must be the key. Awesome.

I make it to the edge of the path leading up to the point. Parish comes down it to meet me halfway.

"This is great! I'm so excited LK is letting us up there. How did that happen?"

He takes me in his arms and stops my questions.

"It's a beautiful morning, isn't it?"

"Gorgeous. You're not having second thoughts about leaving, are you?" I say.

"No, Scarlett. Not about anything."

That last sentence is delivered with a sexy smile and a kiss. We start for the lighthouse. I put on my shoes.

"You're not going to believe what Sam and I found on the way here."

"What?"

"An old bottle that has a rolled up paper stuck in it. I saved it for us to open together."

"A message in a bottle? Oh God! How fun. Didn't Sam want to open it? How'd you manage to hold him back?"

"You kidding? He barely looked at it. Probably a kid rolled up a note and stuck it inside. I'm not getting too excited."

"Let's go see. I brought my cell, so we can get some pictures. That'll make a good one. Sam said his phone was losing battery, and I know you didn't bring yours. See, this is the kind of unexpected thing that comes up. You need to start putting it in your pocket. Plan ahead!" I chuckle.

"I have."

"You've planned ahead?" I say a little confused.

"Quit asking so many questions, woman."

Now I'm intrigued. He leads the way down the narrow path till we're in front of the entry to the lighthouse. He unlocks the red door and stands back to let me pass.

"After you, love."

As soon as I walk through the door my eyes go to the trail of rose petals. They lead from the entry up the spiral metal staircase. I have the strangest feeling in the pit of my stomach. I turn my head to him.

"What's this? I love it," I say, not wanting to read too much into the gesture. But it's hard as hell not to.

"Maybe you should follow them."

So I do. I slowly climb the stairs, savoring each moment of the journey. He's right behind me.

"This is definitely my favorite view," he says. "You should have done this naked."

I ignore his suggestion because I'm so focused on what he's done. When I get to the top of the stairs I hear the soft music. I see the message in the bottle sitting on the ledge, next to his little collection of red sea glass. He's arranged them in the shape of a heart.

And all of it with a hundred and eighty degree view backdrop of the glorious sea seen through the glass. The sun has risen and illuminates the water like sprinkled silver glitter.

But it's just his eyes I want to look at.

Something magical is happening.

"Oh, Parish," is all I can get out.

He walks me to the glass surround and stands behind me. Arms encircle my waist. The glass bottle looks a hundred years old and the paper within just as old. I think it's parchment.

"Why don't you open it," he says softly.

My fingers move over the cool glass, feeling the smooth corner cuts. I expect the cork to be firmly in place, but it comes out easily. Turning the bottle over I shake the tightly rolled message out in my hand. A thin delicate red ribbon holds it together.

A kiss brushes my neck, right under my ear. Chills rush down my spine.

"I love you," he whispers.

"I love you too. I don't know why I'm shaking," I say, knowing exactly why I'm shaking.

Unrolling the parchment I read the message.

Whoever finds this will marry the first person they see.

I'm stunned in the most awesome way. I'm not sure I can speak or move.

"Well you better turn around, babe."

When I turn, hands shaking and tears welling, he's on one knee. My hand lifts to my mouth.

"I waited forty-three years to believe in love, Scarlett. But I'll never doubt again. What I'm asking is, will you marry me?"

I've dreamed of this day. Hoped it would happen. But this. It's beyond any fantasy.

I kneel right in front of him and throw my arms around his neck.

"Yes. Yes! Yes, yes, yes!"

"Is that a yes, Scarlett?"

He starts to laugh, but I silence it with a hundred little kisses, all meant to seal the deal.

ACKNOWLEDGMENTS

Writing seems like a solitary art, but that's not strictly true. There are silent partners in my vision, helpers in league with the dreamer. Invisible hands lifting so I can have a better view of myself. Sharp eyes reading every story told. There are shoulders to stand on so I can see what's possible, letting me know what to aim for. So to all the good-hearted companions in the dream, I say thank you, with an undeniable feeling of gratitude. And to Lara Petterson, who has so steadfastly helped me walk through the fire, I give my love.

ABOUT THE AUTHOR

USA TODAY bestselling author, Leslie Pike, has loved expressing herself through the written word since she was a child. The first romance "book" she wrote was at ten years old. The scene, a California Beach. The hero, a blonde surfer. The ending, happily forever after.

Leslie's passion for film and screenwriting eventually led her to Texas for eight years, writing for a prime time CBS series. She's traveled the world as part of film crews, from Africa to Israel, New York to San Francisco. Now she finds her favorite creative adventures taking place in her home, in Southern California, writing Contemporary Romance.

Connect With Leslie:

Website

Subscribe

FB Readers Group

ALSO BY LESLIE PIKE

The Paradise Series

The Trouble With Eden

Wild In Paradise

The Road To Paradise

The Paradise Box Set

Love In Italy World

The Adventure

The Art Of Love

The Santini Series

Destiny Laughs

Destiny Plays

Destiny Shines

Santini Collection

Destiny Dawns

The Swift Series

The Curve

The Closer

The Cannon

PLAYLIST

"SOMEWHERE OVER THE RAINBOW" – KATHERINE MCPHEE

"WITHOUT YOU – MARIAH CAREY

"HIGH (DUA LIPA) – WHETHAN, DUA LIPA

"RAKSAT SHAHRAZAD (THE DANCE OF SHAHRAZAD) – EMAD SAYYAY

"GOD ONLY KNOWS" – JOHN LEGEND, CYNTHIA ERIVO, YMUSIC

"MY FUNNY VALENTINE" – MILES DAVIS QUINTET

"GRAND AMOUR" – MAISSIAT

"BLUE OCEAN FLOOR" – JUSTIN TIMBERLAKE

"HOW DEEP IS THE OCEAN" – BARBRA STREISAND, JASON GOULD

Made in the USA
San Bernardino, CA
07 January 2020